LOYAL TO THE SOIL 3

Lock Down Publications and Ca$h Presents
Loyal to the Soil 3
A Novel by *Jibril Williams*

Lock Down Publications

P.O. Box 944
Stockbridge, Ga 30281
www.lockdownpublications.com

Copyright 2022 by Jibril Williams
Loyal to the Soil 3

June 2022
Printed in the United States of America

This is a work of fiction. Names, characters, places, and incidents either are products of the author's imagination or are used fictitiously. Any similarity to actual events or locales or persons, living or dead, is entirely coincidental.

Lock Down Publications
Like our page on Facebook: Lock Down Publications @
www.facebook.com/lockdownpublications.ldp

Book interior design by: **Shawn Walker**
Edited by: **Kiera Northington**

Stay Connected with Us!

Text **LOCKDOWN** to 22828 to stay up-to-date with new releases, sneak peaks, contests and more…
Thank you!

Submission Guideline.

Submit the first three chapters of your completed manuscript to ldpsubmissions@gmail.com, subject line: Your book's title. The manuscript must be in a .doc file and sent as an attachment. Document should be in Times New Roman, double spaced and in size 12 font. Also, provide your synopsis and full contact information. If sending multiple submissions, they must each be in a separate email.

Have a story but no way to send it electronically? You can still submit to LDP/Ca$h Presents. Send in the first three chapters, written or typed, of your completed manuscript to:

LDP: Submissions Dept
P.O. Box 944
Stockbridge, Ga 30281

DO NOT send original manuscript. Must be a duplicate.

Provide your synopsis and a cover letter containing your full contact information.

Thanks for considering LDP and Ca$h Presents.

Jibril Williams

Prologue

"What the fuck just happened back there?!" The white woman in six inch heels and wearing a knock off tube fitting Gucci dress thought to herself as she ran and so desperately tried to keep from falling. "OMG! I can't believe what I just saw." Tears threatened to roll down her face. She could hear police sirens in the distance and they were getting closer. Her left heel snapped, sending her stumbling to the pavement. "Aggghhhh!!" she cried out at the ripping of her skin on her hands and knees from hitting the ground with such force. Getting back to her feet, she kicked her heels off, picked them up with her stinging and sore hands, and continued to run. She had to make it off the back streets to her ride that was waiting for her on the Ave. *"I don't know why I let Pretty Ricky talk me into this dumb ass scheme,"* the white woman thought as she ignored the pain in her knees and hands. The Ave. was now just one block away. Two police cars turned onto the street she was running on. She broke her run into a walk. Her heart thumped like an Arabian race horse. She put her head down as the two cop cars approached her with their shining red and blue siren lights.

They shot passed her going in the direction she just came from. She let out a deep breath and turned onto The Ave heading towards Pretty Ricky's waiting car. Pretty Ricky was sitting in his Buick bobbing his head listening to Trey Songz song titled 'Cake' as he waited for his bottom bitch and only bitch to come back from putting a scheme together that he devised. Abruptly his passenger door flew open. It scared the shit out of him. His bottom bitch jumped in the car shaking like a snitch at a gangsta party.

"What the fuck happened to you?" Pretty Ricky asked. "You look like you just bodied a trick or something."

"Please, Pretty Ricky, just drive."

Chapter 1

"Keisha!" Malaya yelled as she chased behind her. Malaya's leg muscles burned as she pumped each one harder trying to catch up with Keisha. Keisha continued to run through the alley without looking back even after she heard her name being called. She was three blocks away from her apartment before looking over her shoulder and watching the female figure chase her. Keisha realized that she still had her 25 automatic in her pocket that her husband Dinkles had given her many years ago. She stopped and turned around to face whoever was chasing her. Malaya breathed heavily through her nose and mouth. Her tongue was bone dry. The warm Florida night and her track and field attempt to catch Keisha had made her sweat fevorlessly and soaked her hijab with sweat. Malaya saw Keisha stop running and turned to face her. Malaya picked up her pace.

"It's over, Keisha!" Malaya yelled, walking up on her out of breath and pointing her 380 with a pearl chrome handle at Keisha. "Stop here," Malaya said with a dry voice. Malaya took a step closer to Keisha and trained the gun to the middle of Keisha's forehead. Keisha seeing that it was Malaya chasing her, made her get a little brave.

"Bitch, you chasing me with a gun knowing damn well you're not going to use it. I'll take that gun from you just like I took that pussy." Keisha took a step closer to Malaya while easing her hand in her pocket.

"Keisha, why? Why all the hate?" Malaya asked.

Before Keisha could reply she responded, "Don't worry about it, Keisha. I'm going to make the sacrifice for my family, so you'll never hurt them again." Keisha saw a look in Malaya's eyes that told her that she was going to die tonight if she didn't make a move for the gun that was in her pocket.

Keisha pulled the small black gun out of her pocket with lightning speed, pointed it at Malaya, and squeezed the trigger. The gun didn't go off. She forgot to put one in the chamber, but Malaya didn't.

Malaya whispered, "Allah Akbar." Then she pulled the trigger on her gun. BOOM! The gun jumped hard in her hand and blew a hole in the middle of Keisha's head.

"Freeze! Drop the gun and lay on the ground." Malaya abruptly woke up, her heart beat against her chest like a bass drum. She sat up on the bunk wiping her sweaty hands on her wrinkled orange jumper. Malaya looked around the small cell. The stainless sink was connected to the stainless toilet, but nothing was stainless about the toilet or sink. They both were covered in all sorts of scum. The cell walls were covered with people's names, neighborhoods, gang names, and gang signs. However, what drove Malaya crazy were the years of black fungus that was growing in the cell corner. Malaya had been in Hillsborough County for the last two days. Tomorrow morning she would be seeing a judge.

Malaya was scared out of her mind, every time she thought about the events that happened two nights ago, she would begin crying and her body began to shake. One of the homicide detectives let her exercise her constitutional right. He gave her only one phone call after Malaya promised to tell him everything that happened and explain why she gunned down her Muslim sister, but after Malaya couldn't get ahold of her husband or her sister Anya, Malaya refused to cooperate with the detectives and opted to remain silent. She requested that her lawyer was present during the interrogation. Malaya wasn't really from the streets, but her husband Velli was and he had taught her well. Malaya got off the small bunk and folded one of the dingy sheets that the C.O. gave her. She placed it on the floor, went over to use the stainless steel sink, and pushed the small hot water button. It was supposed to come out like a rainbow arch, but the water barely came out of the sink high enough to drink out of it due to all the scum that was clogging the faucet. Malaya cupped her hands under the water and began performing Wudu. This is the purification process that every Muslim performs before every prayer which consist of washing the hands, face, arms and feet three times as well as rinsing the mouth and nose out three times.

Malaya would be going to court the following morning. She needed all of the blessings she could get from her creator. She shook water loose from her arms and hands into the sink. Walking back over to where she laid the folded sheet on the floor, she used the sheet to prostrate on when she prayed. Her mind was in a fog. She was second guessing her move on killing Keisha. It was forbidden for one Muslim to kill another Muslim unjustly.

Malaya was uncertain whether or not her action was justified. "Oh, Allah, for me. If I have transgressed bounds beyond my means, please don't place a burden on me greater than I can bare," Malaya whispered to herself as she fought back her tears and prayed.

Jibril Williams

Chapter 2

"This is Angelia McClanahan with The Channel 8 coming to deliver the six o'clock news. We are standing in front of Hillsborough County Jail, where a Muslim woman is being held after she viciously shot another woman by the name of Keisha Leanna Timmons at point blank range in the face in front of Bernard Grant who is Hillsborough County's finest. Now this woman is set to make her first appearance this morning in court." Angelia McClanahan seriously reported the morning news. "We have here Officer Grant, who was the only eyewitness to Mrs. Timmons' murder. Mr. Grant, could you please tell us what you saw the night Mrs. Timmons was shot?" Mrs. McClanahan leaned her Channel 8 mic closer to Officer Grant's lips.

"Well, I cannot answer that at this time. There's still an ongoing investigation."

"Is it true that Keisha was shot two or three streets over from where she lived?"

"Yes, Mrs. McClanahan. That is true. That much I can say."

"My sources tell me that there was a triple homicide committed in the victim's apartment and the Muslim lady that's being held here at this local jail may have committed those murders also." Mr. Grant fidgeted in front of the cameras.

"At this time I cannot confirm that the woman that's being held at this jail had anything to do with the triple homicide that took place on Mulberry Drive."

"Could you tell us the identity of the woman who you saw shoot Mrs. Timmons?" Mrs. McClanahan asked.

"Yes, her name is Malaya Sri Williams. She is a married resident of Wesley Chapel, Florida."

"Do you think this was some type of ISIS attack that was acted out by Malaya Williams?"

"At this point of the investigation, we don't think it was an ISIS attack or an act of terrorism, but the investigation is still ongoing. Mrs. Williams is due in court at 9:30 this morning."

"Okay, there you have it coming live from the Channel 8 News with Angelia McClanahan."

***

Velli watched the morning news with tear threatening eyes and venom in his heart. Malaya, his wife, was in jail facing murder charges. Velli felt like the biggest loser. He felt once again that he failed to protect his wife and keep her out of harm's way. He should have never taken that last minute trip back to D.C. to handle that situation with Stone. Velli placed his head in the palm of his hands and took a deep breath. Damu could feel the tension in the room and if he and Velli didn't have the same blood flowing through their veins, surely he would be dead. "Aye Bruha, my nigga, I'm sorry," Damu said from his leather sofa from across the other side of the living room.

"Sorry don't get my wife out of jail. Sorry doesn't stop my fucking wife from spending the rest of her life in prison." Damu couldn't say anything, he just put his head down and focused on the piece of lint that was planted on his plush black carpet. "Why would you take my wife on a ransom exchange with you, when you know she is not cut for that type of shit?" Velli asked, still holding his head in his hands.

"Bruha, I told you before she wouldn't let us leave her behind. She went crazy when I told her no. I was just thinking of getting my son out of the hands of that bitch Keisha and

14

Stone. I didn't think shit was going to go down the way that it did. I didn't even know that Malaya was strapped. She was supposed to stay in the truck, bruha. I guess when Mike came from out of nowhere spitting that choppa, Biggz made her get out the truck so he could run Mike ass over with the truck, but in the process I guess Malaya saw Keisha trying to get away or some shit and chased her."

"Look, Damu. Fuck all the details of the story. We got to find a way to get my wife out of that jail. I could care less what happened two nights ago. We got to find a way to get Malaya out of that jail before she gets convicted of murder. Even if it comes down to killing her only eyewitness Officer Grant. But right now, we got to get to the court building and see what that judge is talking about," Velli said, shaking his head.

"Alright, Bruha. I'm rolling with you to court," Damu said heading up the stairs to take a shower and get ready for his sister-in-law's first court hearing. "Is the lawyer going to be there?"

"Yeah, I had Anya wire Mr. McCullough fifty thousand out of BAM PUBLICATIONS account for a retainer fee." Damu stopped on the top of the steps.

"Aye bruha, I'm down to handle this any way you see fit, even if we have to go up in that jail and get Malaya ourselves."

Velli just nodded his head up and down, and said,

"It may be the risk that we may have to take."

Chapter 3

"Abdul Hakeem Sabazz. What's your registration number?" the tall black C.O. asked with the large stomach.

"99968-037," Dinkles said his Reg number from memory. He would never forget those eight digit numbers. For the last nine years, the numbers identified who he was and the last three digits of the eight digit number identified where he was from. In the FEDS, every piece of paper you signed your name on you had to attach your eight digit number behind it. No inmate will ever have the same number. They may share the last three digits, but the first five digits will never be the same. "Alright, Mr. Sabazz. Are you going to stay out these crackers human warehouses?" the C.O. asked.

"Yeah, Mr. Baker. I'm going to do whatever it takes for me to stay free."

"Well, you better. You know with that black president in office that you have a lot to be thankful for. I mean that man is freeing more people than slaves, with the new crack laws and clemencies that he has been granting."

"I give all praise to Allah for allowing me to be granted my freedom with the crack law that Mr. Obama has passed through Congress," Hakeem said with a sad tone. Mr. Baker noticed Hakeem's tone.

"Listen, young man. I heard about the situation dealing with your wife. That's some heart breaking shit and it's been all over the news, but don't let that stop you from living. Live for your wife. Do you hear me, Sabazz?"

"Man, why should the fuck I live when everything that I love has died?" Hakeem asked with watery eyes.

"Because you owe it to yourself and your Lord. Now, here. Take your box of clothes that was sent to you for your release and get dressed in the holding cell."

Mr. Baker followed Hakeem to the holding cell and locked him in the holding cell. "Your cab will be here in an hour." Dinkles sat in the R & D (Receive and discharge) Coleman 2 Florida Federal Penitentiary where Dinkles just spent the last 9 ½ years of his life. If it wasn't for the new rule in the Johnson V. United States case where the courts rule that they couldn't enhance you under A.C.C. Arm Career Criminal, he would still be locked up.

The higher courts ruled that it was unconstitutional for the lower courts to enhance a convicted felon that was already sentenced for old crimes he had committed and served time for in the past. If it wasn't for this ruling in the Johnson case, Dinkles would be looking at another ten years in prison. His release should have been one of the happiest days of his life, but it was one of the saddest. Seeing his slain wife's picture flash across the TV screen this morning, shattered his heart in a million pieces. Getting called to the chapel early Saturday morning to be notified by the prison chaplain that his wife was brutally murdered, the chaplain conveyed to him that his deceased wife's mother had called and put the institution on notice that Keisha was dead. The tears roll down Dinkles' face like the levee that broke in New Orleans. Keisha didn't even know that Dinkles was being released from prison. He wanted to write her and let her know, but he wanted it to be a surprise. Dinkles' hands trembled as he pulled the last letter that his wife wrote him out of his pocket. He received the letter two days ago. It had been almost two years since Keisha had written him. He took a deep breath as he unfolded the letter and began to read his wife's last words to him.

"As-Salam-u-Alaikum, Hakeem,

I know that it has been a long time since I have written you a letter, and I must say that I deeply apologize for neglecting you. That's no way for a wife to be treating her husband.

Especially, after all that you have done for me in the past. I'm writing asking you for your forgiveness. I know that I don't deserve it, but I'm asking anyway. Hakeem, baby. Can you please forgive me? I just need another week, and all the bad times will be behind me. There's so much I need to confess to you to make things right, so you can know what I've been going through without you. I realize no one cares and understands me but you. Just give me another week and I promise I won't miss another visiting day, just one more week. In the meantime, I put $10, 000 on your account. I love you, Hakeem. I'll be seeing you soon.

Love your Wife,

Keisha

Dinkles folded the letter back up, placed it back in his pocket, and got dressed and ready for the world.

Chapter 4

Anya watched as the small beads of sweat built on her son's forehead while he slept next to her. Anya wiped the sweat from his forehead with her thumb. She worried gravely about her three year old son. Ever since she had gotten Tiriq back from his kidnappers, he had been sucking his thumb when he slept. The beads of sweat formulated on his forehead as if he was having a nightmare. Anya desperately wanted to take her son to get some medical treatment, but with the three bodies that were left on Mulberry Drive it was impossible to do so without taking the chance of being linked to the murders.

The last thing Tiriq needed was for his mother to go to jail for a murder beef. Anya wiped her eyes with the corner of her pillow case, placed a small kiss on the top of Tiriq's head, and whispered in her son's ear, "It's going to be alright, little man. Momma got you."

The only thing that came out of Tiriq's abduction was Tiriq's urge to talk. Before he was kidnapped, Tiriq never said one word to a living soul. Anya was grateful that she now could get small conversations out of her son, but when she asked him about the bad people that took him, Tiriq would go into his mental cocoon and stop talking for hours at a time. Anya let out a sigh and palmed Tiriq's small hand inside of hers. She was happy to have her baby back home resting beside her in her bed. Tiriq was held captive for about fourteen days. Those fourteen days were a nightmare for Anya. Every day without Tiriq, Anya wanted to die. When Tiriq was gone, she kept telling herself that she couldn't lose another child, after losing her daughter Ai'day. Anya could still hear that one fatal gunshot that stole her daughter away from her forever. Anya wiped more sweat from Tiriq's forehead. Now with having Tiriq back in her presence, she was ready to leave Florida.

Too much happened since she'd been living in the sunshine state, but she couldn't leave without Malaya. She couldn't believe that Malaya killed Keisha right in front of a police officer. *"What the hell was she thinking?"* Anya thought to herself. She never thought Malaya had what it takes to kill someone, especially someone like Keisha. Someone that once was so close to her.

Checking the clock which read 7:45 a.m., Anya knew in the next two hours that Malaya was due in court. Anya's better judgement told her not to step foot into that courtroom, but the love and loyalty that resided in her heart for Malaya demanded that she support her sister and partner in crime. Anya eased out of bed, careful not to wake Tiriq. Her body ached from the built up tension her body endured over the past few weeks. Anya headed to the bathroom. Reaching for the shower, she turned the hot and cold nobs to adjust the shower to her liking. Stripping out her t-shirt and panties stepping into the shower, the hot water massaged her neck. Anya was hoping that the shower would help clear her mind, but she was sadly mistaken. Her thoughts drifted back to Malaya. She hoped that her beloved sister was remaining strong, but a piece of Anya felt that Malaya wasn't strong enough to withstand the type of pressure that the police would put her under. The type of integration that the police put you under dealing with murder wasn't a joke. Anya doubted in her mind that Malaya would hold strong about the murders that took place on Mulberry Drive. "Damn, Malaya. Please stick to the "G" code," Anya spoke to herself as she lathered her body.

Chapter 5

"Mrs. Williams!" The white guard called Malaya's name from the outside the holding cell.

"Yes," Malaya replied, getting off the bunk and approaching the holding cell's door.

"It's court time," the guard said, unlocking the cell door with a skeleton key. When the guard turned the key in the door, it made a hard thud sound that almost made Malaya jump out of her skin. Malaya stepped out the cell to be greeted by a female guard that wore a Hillsborough County Correctional uniform with a name tag with Jones on it. "Stand right there, ma'am. Turn around and place your hands behind your back." Malaya complied with Ms. Jones' orders. She placed the handcuffs on Malaya's small wrist. Ms. Jones and the white C.O. led Malaya down a small well lit hallway and made a stop at a door that read R & D (Receive & discharge). This was the same room that Malaya came through two nights ago. "Crack R & D," the white C.O. ordered through his radio. Seconds later, the R & D door popped open with a buzzing sound. Malaya and her two escorts entered.

Un-cuffing Malaya at the R & D desk, Ms. Jones and the other guard left the room leaving Malaya with the Big Precious look alike that was sitting behind the desk staring. She said, "I hate you pretty bitches. Name!" The Precious look alike sounded off with a no respect in her voice.

"Hmmm, Ma-Malaya Williams."

"Number!"

"275-942." Malaya recited the number that was scribbled across her jail issued arm band. It was issued to her the first night she stepped foot in the hell hole.

"Okay," the Precious look alike said, walking around the desk and slipping on a pair of green latex gloves. "Now strip!"

Big Precious yelled as she stopped in front of Malaya. It hit Malaya that she had to endure the same procedure that she went through two days ago. Malaya had to strip in front of another female officer when she first came through R & D Friday night. The only thing that's different from Friday night and now was that two days ago she had to strip in front of a room full of women. They made her run her fingers through her hair and bend over at the waist and spread her butt cheeks. The female officer took a peep to determine if she had any contraband hidden in her anal cavity. Malaya's eyes watered over just thinking about the humiliation that she went through.

"Look, bitch! You make it hard for me. I'll make it hard for you," the big Precious look alike said, getting in Malaya's face. Malaya slowly pulled her hijab off and handed it to the guard, which she snatched from Malaya and aggressively searched it. "I don't know why you acting all timid. You wasn't acting timid when you killed that poor girl in front of Officer Grant."

The words stung Malaya like salt thrown in a fresh wound. Malaya didn't respond to fatso's comment. She didn't even make eye contact with the guard. She just went through the motions of exposing all the goods to the guard. Putting back on her clothes, Big Precious radio'd for Malaya's escort. Three large police officers came through a side door wearing black cargo pants and laced up black combat boots tied tight around the ankles. All of them were equipped with bullet proof vest and walkie talkies. One of the officers threw a bullet proof vest at Malaya's torso.

"What I need a vest for?" Malaya questioned with concern. "I'm going to court not a war."

"Oh. You don't know yet, huh?" one of the white officers asked. "You are the new American Gangster." The officer that

24

was fitting Malaya for the vest bust out laughing at his partner's little joke. The officer clamped the cuffs on Malaya's wrists and placed shackles around her ankles. The feeling that the shackles and handcuffs gave Malaya was degrading and made her feel less than human. She felt like a slave.

"This must be how Velli felt all those years that he was incarcerated." Just thinking about her husband made her heart race for his love. "Okay, let's go!" one of the police officers said heading out the door. Malaya could barely walk in the shackles on her ankles and had to match the officers pace to keep up with the ones leading the way down the hallway. They stopped at a control booth where the officers retrieved their 9mm guns and placed them in the holsters.

"Let's do this!" one of the police said as he stopped at a door in front of the control booth. Two officers stood on opposite sides of Malaya and nodded their heads up and down in agreement. The leading officer gave the control booth commander a hand wave and the door buzzed. The leading guard pushed the door and stepped through it. Malaya followed behind the officer and once she stepped outside, everything around her lit up with flashing cameras. Every news station that she could think of was outside Hillsborough County Jail snapping pictures of her with all types of microphones and recording devices shoved in her face.

"Mrs. Williams, why did you kill Keisha Timmons?" the news reporter asked, holding a Channel 8 microphone up to Malaya's mouth, trying to capture every word if Malaya had anything to say. "Did you have anything to do with the murders that took place in Keisha's apartment on Mulberry Drive?"

"Are you a terrorist?" another reporter shouted out. Malaya tried to shield her face, but it was useless due to her hands being handcuffed and chained to her waist. The officers kept pushing past the mob of reporters. Malaya was placed in a Hillsborough County police car and rushed off to the court building.

Chapter 6

Mango took a pull of his cigar while he swirled the whiskey around in his glass. Mango had been drinking non-stop by himself for the last three hours. His thinning hair was plastered to his head from the sweat that ran down his head. The sweat dripped from his face and soaked the front of his shirt. For the last five days, Mango's world had been hell. He shipped a hundred keys to Washington, D.C. to one of his distributors named Stone. That was four days ago. In return, Stone was to have his brother Mookie deliver the money to him in Texas. After the drop was made, he never heard from Stone or his brother Mookie. To add injury to insult, Mango sent another shipment to another distributor named Mike in South Beach, Florida. Mike never showed up to pick the product up. Now he had the cartel in Mexico breathing down his back about the non-moving product and the sudden decrease in money flow on his end. "Puta muthafuka's," Mango spoke out loud. "I should have never dealt with them black monkey mutha-fuka's." The Mexican Cartel gives strict orders not to do busi-ness with the blacks. They thought that it was bad for business to deal with the blacks because they are too flashy and drive foreign cars in deprived neighborhoods. They never take their money to rebuild the communities. It was like the money made the blacks worse off as a person. The sad part about the blacks was they killed each other over the crumbs they made in the streets. What really made doing business with the blacks forbidden was, they couldn't be trusted to keep their mouths closed. When one of the blacks got caught doing their dirt, they always snitched to the Feds. Mango knew he was in deep shit and if he didn't find Stone and Mookie and find out what the hell was going on with Mike, he was going to die a terrible death. Mango let out the cigar smoke through his nose, and his body got engulfed in goose bumps just thinking about what the Sicario Cartel would do to him for losing a hundred keys and dealing with the blacks. He was going to have to take a trip to D.C. to see if he could locate Stone and Mookie. Then maybe slide down to Florida to pay Velli a visit, and hopefully, he would get a chance to find out what was going on with Mike. He felt that Mike was in Tampa trying to get revenge on Velli for killing his wife. Velli and Damu left Mike for dead, but thanks to Mike wearing a vest and Velli's poor shooting skills, Mike escaped with a broken collarbone and grazed cheek. Velli and Damu didn't have a clue that Mike was still alive. So, Mango set Mike up in South Beach running his South Beach operation. Mango forbid Mike to step foot back into Tampa. Mango saw an opportunity. He put the press game down on Velli at his wedding, threatening to kill his entire family unless Velli continued to fill Mike's shoes in Tampa. Velli agreed only if Mango supplied him in Washington, D.C. also. Mango made a deal with Velli and Velli had been moving drugs for him ever since. *"Mike must've gotten tired sitting in South Beach waiting on him to give him the green light to go to Tampa to reclaim his city and revenged his wife's death,"* Mango thought to himself. Mike was too loyal to abandon ship on him. Mango downed the glass of whiskey. "Fuck it. I'm going to D.C."

Chapter 7

Malaya sat in the bullpen at The Hillsborough County court building. She and about forty other female prisoners were cramped into the holding cell. It was really fit to hold 20 people or so. All the body odors assaulted the holding cell. Malaya's nostrils and eyes burned from the smell. Malaya never knew so many people could smell so bad, and it didn't help that a brown-skinned chick was laying two feet away from her. The chick was detoxing from her long life of heroin use. She had just shitted and pissed all over herself. Malaya wanted to throw up so bad because of the stench. Malaya sat on the concrete slab bench that hurt her tailbone. A light-skinned woman kept eye fucking her with dirty looks. The girl had a short Caesar cut like Amber Rose. Her dark brown eyes highlighted her light skin tone. The black one piece tight fitted Prada dress hugged her curves to a "T." Malaya could tell that the girl was a high-priced hooker or a stripper that was strictly about her paper. Malaya avoided eye contact with the girl. She didn't want any more trouble than what she was in already. "Malaya Williams!" one of the sheriffs called from the front of the holding cell.

"Yeah!" Malaya answered from the back of the cell.

"Come on. Your lawyer is here to see you." Malaya got up, making her way to the front of the cell, where the sheriff was waiting for her. Malaya tried her best not to brush up on anyone. She swore that everyone smelled like shit and period juice. Making it to the waiting sheriff that held the cell door open, Malaya stepped out, making eye contact for the first time with the woman in the Prada dress. Malaya needed to remember her face in case she ran into her later on down the road. "Okay, hands out," the sheriff ordered, and placed handcuffs on Malaya's wrist.

"OMG!" the female sheriff said, fanning her nose. "You bitches stink like shit. You bitches need a serious shower." That comment set the women in the cage off. "Fuck you, bitch!" one of the women yelled from the holding cell.

"You nappy head whore!" another one yelled out. The sheriff just laughed, throwing her middle finger up in the air as she led Malaya down the corridor. Stopping at a metal door, the sheriff unlocked the door and Malaya stepped inside.

The room was cold and filthy. It was divided by plexiglass. There were eight or nine cement stools in front of the plexiglass for inmates to sit on while they talked to their lawyers on a phone that hung from a metal bar that was in the middle of the plexiglass, giving each stool a phone of its own. A small blond headed white woman was waiting for Malaya. The sheriff closed the door behind her. The white woman waved Malaya over to the glass where the phone was. Malaya grabbed the phone. "Hello."

"Malaya Williams?" The woman asked, shuffling through some papers in the front of her.

"Yes, that's me."

"Okay, I'm your lawyer. My name is Lisa Flowers. I have been appointed by the courts to represent you in your court matter. Okay, I'm looking here and see that you're here for the murder of Keisha Timmons." Mrs. Flowers looked up from her papers at Malaya. "Also, it says that you were caught with the murder weapon, which was a chrome 380 hand gun and that you killed Ms. Timmons in front of a Hillsborough County police officer. Mrs. Williams, is this true?" the lawyer asked, not really believing what she read off the paperwork she had on Malaya.

"Yes, that's true," Malaya agreed.

"Mrs. Williams, tell me what happened."

Malaya dropped her head. She knew that she couldn't tell this woman why she killed Keisha. To do so, she would have to mention Tiriq's kidnapping and the murders that took place in Keisha's apartment. She couldn't do that. She made a sacrifice to protect her loved ones. "No, I cannot tell you what happened. It just happened," Malaya replied.

"Okay, that's your call, but you know that we will not win this case with the sheriff being an eyewitness to your crime. They have the murder weapon with your fingerprints all over it. This case will be impossible to win. So, you need to get in front of the judge and plead guilty to all charges. Ask the court to have mercy on you on sentencing day." Malaya knew that she could not win the case. Mrs. Flowers was right. They had the murder weapon with her prints on it, and Officer Grant was an eyewitness to the killing.

Malaya thought to herself, *"Allah, whatever happens to me is your creed."*

"Okay, I will plead guilty to all charges," Malaya said with drones in her mouth.

"Okay, that will work and is best for all parties," Mrs. Flowers said. However, she was really thinking about herself. The public defender service receives 1,500 per case. The quicker she got the case over with, the sooner she could obtain her money. She possibly could even get a bonus for getting Malaya to cop-out and save the government some money for not having to take Malaya to trial. "Okay, Mrs. Williams. I will have the sheriff come get you and bring you upstairs to the courtroom." Malaya nodded her head. The lawyer left and ten minutes later, the same female sheriff came and got her from out of the legal visiting room. Malaya walked in the courtroom. She felt everyone's eyes on her. It seemed that the AC was on extra high. An icy chill shot through her body. The courtroom was packed with reporters and camera crews.

"Damn, they blowing this thing up," Malaya thought to herself. She scanned the courtroom for Velli or any of her loved ones. Her heart dropped when she didn't see Velli, Damu or Anya. Taking her place next to her public defender Lisa Flowers, her court proceedings began. "I'm Judge Karen Jackson. I will be on the case of Malaya Williams vs United States."

"I'm Lisa Flowers from the public defender's service office, and I'll represent Mrs. Williams in this matter."

"I'm U.S. Attorney Samantha Davis and I will be prosecuting this case." The red head freckled face woman said with confidence.

"So, what do we have?" the judged asked.

"We have one case of first degree murder. The victim was Keisha Timmons," Mrs. Davis sounded off. "Mrs. Williams shot the victim in front of a Hillsborough County police officer. Mr. Bernard Grant, also Mr. Grant recovered the murder weapon with Mrs. Williams' fingerprints on it." Judge Karen Davis looked at Malaya with hatred. Malaya couldn't maintain eye contact with the judge, so she dropped her head in submission.

"Mrs. Flowers, how does your client plea?" the judge sternly asked.

"My client pleads guilty, Your Honor-"

"Hold up. Sorry to interrupt, Your Honor." A brown-skinned man stepped forward in his black Tom Ford suit. "My name is Leon McCullough and I was retained by the Williams family this morning to represent Mrs. Williams. Sorry about my tardiness, but the traffic was heavy coming in this morning," Mr. McCullough said, stepping up next to Malaya. The judge gave him the evil eye.

"Well, we are happy to have you. Mrs. Flowers, thank you. You can be excused." The sellout lawyer slammed her brief-case shut and made her way out of the courtroom. She was mad that she wouldn't be receiving the 1,500 dollars for handling Malaya's case. Malaya turned and watched the public defender leave. She caught a glimpse of Velli, Damu and Anya standing in the back of the courtroom. Malaya smiled seeing her king. Velli blew her a kiss and mouthed the words, I Love You. Seeing her husband, Malaya felt stronger.

"Mr. McCullough, I want to inform you that your client had chosen to plead guilty in this case."

"Your Honor, please may I have a quick word with my client?"

"Go ahead, Mr. McCullough. You have five minutes."

"Listen, Mrs. Williams. Withdraw your guilty plea," McCullough said, looking into Malaya's eyes. Malaya didn't understand.

"But McCullough, I did this. I killed Keisha."

"It doesn't matter, let me try to find you away out of this situation. Let me work my mojo if I can," Mr. McCullough whispered into Malaya's ear. Malaya felt like she could trust her lawyer.

"Okay, I will withdraw the plea."

"Your Honor, after talking with my client she wishes to withdraw her guilty plea and she wishes to plead not guilty."

The courtroom went into an uproar. Judge Jackson banged her gavel. "Order in my court!" The court room became quiet. "Mr. McCullough, you and your client understand the charges that Mrs. Williams is faced with?"

"Yes, Your Honor. We both do, and I think I would be an unfit lawyer if I let my client plead guilty to this crime without at least having a mental evaluation done on her to see if my client is fit to stand trial for this crime."

"Okay, Mr. McCullough. Not guilty it is. We'll come back in 120 days for a status hearing and see if the government will have an indictment for Mrs. Williams." Mr. McCullough wrote a few things down on his legal pad.

"Okay, Your Honor. We agree on that. I would like to request a bond hearing."

"You can have the bond hearing when we come back for the status hearing, until then Mrs. Williams will remain in custody." With that said, the sheriff led Malaya out of the courtroom. Looking back at Velli, he mouthed the words 'Be Strong' at Malaya.

Chapter 8

Hakeem rode in the backseat of the yellow cab in silence. It had been nine long years since he was a free man and the saying, "Time waits for no one," is true because everything on the outside looked so different from the last time he could remember. The cars, the way people dressed, the whole scenery was different. The outside world seemed dull. Hakeem wondered was it because the only person who brought any type of light in his life was now none existent. Hakeem tightly clenched his fist and laid his head on the headrest. The cab driver watched Hakeem through his rearview mirror.

"How you doing back there, son?" the cab driver asked the question, interrupting Hakeem's thoughts.

"I'm fine."

"How long have you been on the inside?"

Hakeem sighed. "Nine years and nine months."

"Wow, welcome back, son," the old black man said over his shoulder. "Often I pick guys up from prison and drive them to the airport or bus station, and they always tell me how much things have changed and how different things look. When every last one of them is released, they're excited to be free from the belly of the beast, but you don't seem excited at all."

"I'm excited. I just lost someone that was close to me and I been waiting nine longs years to make it home to them just so they could die two days before my release." The cab driver couldn't say nothing. He just focused on driving. Hakeem pulled a photo out of his pocket of Keisha standing in front of Masjid ISTABA with Anya and Malaya. The trio looked so happy and full of life wrapped in hijabs. Hakeem wondered what really happened between the three sisters. They were so close and well knitted. *"Why would Malaya kill Keisha?"* Hakeem thought to himself, placing the photo back in his pocket and laying his head back on the headrest, closing his eyes for the rest of the ride. The yellow cab driver stopped his cab in front of a yellow and white house on Eagle View Drive in Brandon. "Yo, my man, we are here!" the cab driver yelled over his shoulder bringing Hakeem out his light slumber. Hakeem wiped the sleep out of his eyes and retrieved a small wad of cash that was given to him by the institution. He requested that the institution give him $500 in cash and the rest of the $10,000 that Keisha sent him be placed on a Chase card for him.

"How much?" Hakeem asked.

"$90 bucks."

"Damn, I see why you often pick the prisoners up from the prison."

"Hey, man. A guy got to feed his family." The cab driver chuckled. Hakeem handed a $100 bill to the cab driver and told him to keep the change. He stood in front of the yellow house with a bag of pictures and old letters that he accumulated over the years. Hakeem checked the address on the envelope of the last letter that Keisha wrote him. *"This is it,"* Hakeem thought to himself and he made his way up to the front door of the house. Taking a deep breath, Hakeem knocked on the door. He didn't know what he was going to say, or if he even knew the people that lived at the address.

Moments later, the door opened and Hakeem stood staring in the eyes of Keisha's mother. "Alhamdulillah!" She screamed out, wrapping her arms around Hakeem's neck and squeezing him tight. "As-Salam-u-Alaikum, Hakeem."

"Wa Alaikum Salaam Ummi (Mother) Ms. Timmons, I didn't know where else to go." Hakeem stumbled over his words.

"You came to the right place, and hush with the Ms. Timmons and call me Fatima. Please come in, I just got back from Malaya's court hearing.

***

Splash rode the other end of the double headed 12 inch dildo like an expert horse jockey. Peaches had the other end of the menacing looking love toy buried in her pussy. She worked her hips viciously, trying to keep up with Splash's rhythm. The two women had been going at it for the last forty-five minutes. Splash called Peaches over to help relieve her of some stress. Splash was planning to skip out of town with her baby father's brother named Stone. They were planning on going to Paris after Stone's retiring out the game party. But after the party, Stone never came home and her baby's father named Mookie was nowhere to be found. "OOOOOOOH! Yes!" Splash moaned as she was about to cum all over the big black love toy. "Fuck me!" Splash jumped up and down on the plastic dick with a mean mug on her face, biting down hard on her bottom lip. Her heart was in turmoil that Stone didn't keep his word and take her with him. *"I bet that him and Mookie together in Paris with some dirty ass bitches,"* Splash thought to herself as she felt her orgasm begin to come to a head. Knock-knock-knock. A knock came from the front door. Splash ignored the knock and kept on coating the dildo with her juices. She knew that whoever it was knocking could hear her and Peaches getting their freak on, so hopefully they would go away. However, Splash was wrong. The person that was at the door kept knocking and broke her concentration. "No, Splash. Don't stop. I'm about to cum," Peaches said with a frown on her face from the other end other the dildo.

"Whoever is knocking is fucking up my concentration," Splash said, easing off the dildo and went over to the door with no clothes on and no regards for whoever knocked on the door. "What!" Splash swung the door open, exposing her butt naked body, and making eye contact with a fat Spanish man.

"Yes, I'm looking for a Stone or Mookie," the Spanish man stated while eyeing Splash's goodies. Splash looked past the man and could see the white on white 600 double-parked in front of her and Mookie's house.

"And, who the fuck is you?"

"I'm Mango." Splash knew the name, but never saw the face. Many times when she was with Stone, she'd be sucking his dick while he held conversations on the phone with a guy he called Mango.

"You mean that you are the supplier?" Splash knew that he wanted to taste her forbidden fruit. Splash's money hungry wheels turned.

"Mango, come in, please. I haven't seen Mookie or Stone in days, but I do have something that I want to show you," Splash said with a devilish smile.

Chapter 9

Malaya had a helluva day. She was so tired when she got back from court. The mob of news reporters and camera crews was unbelievable. Malaya knew that her picture must've been taken a million times from a million different angles. She wouldn't be spending a few days in a holding cell by herself. She was going to be processed into the jail and be placed in general population with one hundred and twenty-five other women. Arriving back at Hillsborough County Jail, Malaya was taken to R & D. There were about sixty women there that just came back from court waiting to be processed into the jail. Malaya was placed in a holding cell with the other sixty women. Just like the courthouse holding cell, it reeked of funky ass and feet. Malaya found a corner to stand in. The cell was jam packed. Breathing through her mouth, Malaya wondered did she make the right decision by killing Keisha. The truth was, things didn't feel any different from when Keisha was alive. *"Is this how Allah is telling me that my actions were not justified?"* Malaya asked herself. *"I can't worry about this right now. I got to focus on my situation here at this jail,"* Malaya thought. Malaya scanned the room. Her body shook looking at the women that were held captive with her. Episodes of Lock Up invaded her thoughts, and hives grew all over her body just thinking about some of the things she'd seen on TV. Tightly balling her fist, Malaya thought to herself that if she could talk to her husband, she would be alright. Seeing Velli earlier in court lifted her spirits, but she needed to hear his voice and seek his advice.

"As Salaam Alaikum!" Malaya turned to the woman that greeted her, making eye contact with the tallest woman that she had ever seen. "My name is Akeemah," the large, shapely woman said as she extended her hand. Malaya was hesitant, but the sister did greet her with "Peace be upon you." So, Malaya accepted Akeemah's hand.

"Wa Alaikum Salaam. I'm Malaya."

"Is this your first time being in jail?" Akeemah questioned.

"Is it that obvious?" Malaya shot back while checking her surroundings, seeing if anyone was watching her.

"Yeah, sister. It's that obvious." Akeemah smiled.

"So are you Muslim or you just know that greeting?" Malaya asked.

"Yeah, I'm Muslim. I'm just struggling with my faith." Looking Akeemah over you would never guess that she was Muslim with her skin tight jeans hugging every curve and the Michael Kor blouse that showed too much cleavage. Nevertheless, the 6'3 woman was beautiful. She had hips and ass for days, and with her light brown eyes, she could humble a man of any size.

"So, is this your first time being in jail?" Malaya asked, feeling a little comfortable with Akeemah. Akeemah made a sad face and her eyes glazed over the tears.

"No, girl. This is not my first rodeo," Akeemah said with sadness in her eyes. "Hopefully, this will be my last time." Before Malaya could ask Akeemah what she was locked up for, a plump female officer opened the holding cell door and started calling names.

"Latrici Coleman, Deshawn Obir, Malaya Williams, Akeemah Ali." Malaya was grateful that Akeemah was called out with her.

"What they call all of us out for?" Malaya asked Akeemah, looking frightened.

"They are going to take our pictures, fingerprint us, and take us to the infirmary to get checked out. Then we will be assigned housing units. We are in for a long night. The process takes forever." Malaya just shook her head and followed the group of women out of the holding cell. The process was humiliating for Malaya. She had to strip down into her nakedness again in front of the group of women. She was asked to viciously run her fingers through her hair, then she was asked to lift her breasts up, turn around, bend at the waist, and spread her ass cheeks. Malaya felt like every ounce of dignity was stripped away from her. The whole time she was going through this torment, her eyes threatened to water like a stormy night. She wanted to buck the whole process, but after seeing a woman beaten and pepper sprayed right in front of her own eyes for refusing to obey a direct order from the officer and strip like the officer asked her to do, she changed her mind. Akeemah sensed that Malaya had an issue with the strip search. She had to whisper to Malaya, "Sister, don't let them hurt you. Go through with the search. It will be over soon. However, she knew the scars of embarrassment would be forever on Malaya's heart and mind. From there, an officer escorted Malaya, Akeemah, and the rest of the women to the infirmary where they were asked a string of questions about their medical history and sex life. "Have you ever had chicken pox, herpes, or are you H.I.V positive?" The questions were asked non-stop. Malaya answered every question with frustration. Malaya saw the P.A for her blood work. They drew blood and requested for her to urinate in a small bottle. Malaya was so overwhelmed with the whole pissing in the bottle situation. She managed to fill the bottle up, but pissed all over her hand. Handing the P.A back the urine sample, Malaya went next door to see the psychologist. Malaya was in and out the psychologist's office so fast she couldn't even tell you what the doctor looked like. Malaya sat next to Akeemah on the bench in the infirmary.

"So, where we go from here?" Malaya asked, mouth dry and dog ass tired.

"Well, our next stop is our housing unit, then it's doing time until we go back to court. I hope that we end up in the same housing unit," Akeemah said, resting her head on the wall and closing her eyes. The thought of her being separated from Akeemah scared Malaya. For some reason, Akeemah brought Malaya some comfort. "Okay ladies, dykes, and pussy lickers. Grab a bed roll and follow me," a C.O. said, trying to be funny. The women grabbed a bed roll and followed the C.O. to the second floor of the jail. Malaya prayed. "Oh, Allah. Whatever block that I end up in, please send Akeemah with me."

They stopped in front of cell block B. "Okay, if I call your name, this will be your temporary home until you are released or otherwise," the C.O. stated. "Keysha Hanes, Tawanna Wallace, Crystal Tyler, and Kia Wright!" the C.O. yelled a bunch of names off. Malaya was holding her breath the whole time, hoping that she and Akeemah's name wouldn't be called so they wouldn't be split up. Akeemah sensed that, and she held Malaya's hand in the process. "Okay, the rest of you bitches will be going to cell block C down the hall." Malaya thanked Allah as she and Akeemah were escorted down the hall to C-block.

Chapter 10

Velli laid wide awake in his bed, thoughts of Malaya wouldn't let him rest. Visions of her handcuffed and shackled, standing in that courtroom rattled him. The expressions that Malaya wore on her face today were of a frightened little kid. All he could do was smile at his wife and mouth the words, I Love You to her to try to bring her some type of reassurance that he was there for her. He reached over to the empty space where Malaya used to lay next to him. Velli balled the cold sheet into his fists. The coconut Channel no. 5 fragrance that floated off Malaya's pillow case made him crave for his wife more. *"This must be how Malaya felt those nine years I was locked up,"* Velli thought to himself. Velli thought how he and Malaya's roles had reversed. Malaya waited nine years for him while he was locked up, now he waited as his wife once did. He hoped that Malaya would have a different ending than he did, but he knew that it was far-fetched. She murdered Keisha in front of a Hillsborough County police officer. Just that thought alone made Velli's body shiver. "Dammit! Malaya, what was you thinking?" Velli whispered to himself. Velli felt as though he failed as a husband, and he let his wife down. There was no way that he was supposed to run off to D.C. to handle Stone's rat ass when his family was in a crisis. Velli let out a deep breath of frustration as he wiped the falling tears from his face. "Oh, Allah! I know that I haven't been the best of your servants, but why punish Malaya with hardships and not me? I'm the one who has made transgressions against you," Velli spoke out loud, swinging his feet over the side of the queen size bed, alerting the huge blue breed pit named Wicket. Wicket cried like a baby. All of the love he had for Malaya came pouring out through his tears.

***

"Hakeem, I got to get some rest. The morgue released Keisha's body over to the Masjid. I'm making preparations for her janazah service (Islamic burial) in two days," Fatima said, heading up the stairs to her room. "You can make yourself comfortable in the guest room."

"Okay, Ummi. (Mom)

"I love when you call me mom, Hakeem. I'm so happy that you came here once you got released." Fatima smiled bright at Hakeem and made her way up the stairs for bed. Hakeem sat in the living room thinking about the past events Keisha's mom revealed to him. He couldn't believe that Malaya and Anya barged in her house waving guns looking for Keisha and when they didn't find Keisha in the house, they tied Fatima up, hunted her daughter down the same night, and killed her like a dog. The next day, when two officers came to notify Fatima that her daughter had been killed, they found her tied up on the living room floor. *"What the hell gotten into Malaya and Anya? Why is Malaya locked up and not Anya?"* Hakeem thought to himself. Hakeem would give anything to hold his wife in his arms again. He knew that Keisha was out there doing her thing in the streets, but Keisha was his wife and no one had the right to take her away from him. Keisha was who opened his heart to love. If it wasn't for the fact that Malaya was Muslim, he would've been out there killing everything that she loved. The only person who Malaya loved that Hakeem knew of was Velli. Hakeem couldn't hurt Velli. He had too much love for his brother,but Shaton was definitely in his ear to seek revenge for his wife's death. Hakeem made his way up the stairs to the guest room. He stopped in Keisha's room and stepped inside of it. He could tell that the room was a female heaven. The room was decorated in pink and white. The queen size bed was made nice and neat. He could tell that no one had slept in the bed in a while. Walking over to Keisha's dresser, he spotted a picture of him and Keisha on their wedding day. That day was one of the happiest days of Hakeem's life. He stared at the picture. He could see Keisha's happiness and the love beamed through the picture. He would do anything to be able to touch his wife's chocolate skin again and smell her. He suddenly remembered that Keisha's mom told him that Keisha came by the house the morning that she died. She was carrying a bag full of clothes. She told her mother that she needed somewhere to store her clothes until she moved into her new apartment. Fatima, knowing her daughter, knew Keisha had more belongings than what she was carrying, but she didn't want to pry. She was just happy to see her daughter. Hakeem looked around the room for the bag, hoping he could find an item that belonged to Keisha that held her scent. Seeing a black strap sticking from under the bed, it seemed somewhat odd for Keisha to store her clothes under the bed. Hakeem grabbed the strap and pulled a black gym bag from under the bed. He sat on the bed and stared at it. *"What is this? It's not clothes,"* Hakeem said to himself as he unzipped the bag and the stacks of money spilled out onto the floor. "What the fuck! Baby, what have you gotten yourself into?" Hakeem spoke to himself. He picked up a few stacks of bills and thumbed through the money. Hundred dollar bills after hundred dollar bills flipped through his hands. Seeing this money, he knew that his wife was in some serious shit. He wondered if that was how Keisha sent him that $10,000 before he got out of prison. *"What did Malaya have to do with this money for her to kill Keisha?"* Hakeem thought to himself as he tried to piece his wife's death together. Placing the money back into the bag and walking over to Keisha's dresser again, he opened the top drawer. Nicely folded panties laid in the drawer. Hakeem ran his hand over a pair of silk cherry colored lace thongs. He picked them up and smelled them, trying to get a whiff of Keisha's scent, but his wife's scent was lost to Tide with Bleach. Digging deeper into the drawer, Hakeem felt something hard. As he moved the extra layer of panties out of the way, Hakeem's eyes fell on an old friend of his. It was a 357 python. He couldn't believe that Keisha kept his gun after all those years. The gun felt heavy and odd in his hand. Opening the cylinder on the gun, six large shells rested nicely in the gun. "Damn, these bullets are old," Hakeem whispered, closing the cylinder on the gun and putting it on his waistband. Seeing an envelope at the bottom of the drawer, Hakeem retrieved it and opened it. Two pictures stared at him of Keisha with the reddest dude he had ever seen and another picture of a fly guy. He could tell the dude was getting some major money by the jewels he wore around his neck. He and Keisha were hugged up, but so was she and the red dude in the other picture. Hakeem placed the pictures in his pocket, closed his wife's drawer, and left the room. He had a lot on his mind. He had to find out who were the two dudes in the pictures with Keisha. He had a feeling they would lead him to why Malaya killed his wife.

Chapter 11

"Malaya!" Malaya's cellmate Jada woke her up from her deep sleep. The trip from court and the whole process into the jail drained her. Malaya and Akeemah were able to make it into the same block together, but they weren't lucky enough to be placed in the same cell together. Malaya was in cell 36 and Akeemah was placed in cell 38.

"What time is it, Jada?" Malaya asked.

"It's about 3:30 or 4 a.m. It's breakfast time, we got to get our trays," Jada said, putting her shoes on.

"Who eats breakfast at 4 a.m. in the morning?" Malaya complained, just then her stomach let out a grumble that was loud enough to wake the dead. She realized that she had not eaten at all yesterday. Malaya jumped up and brushed her teeth with the institution's toothpaste that was rolled up in her bed roll that she received last night. The fresh mint toothpaste was horrible. There wasn't nothing fresh or mint about it. Malaya thoroughly rinsed her mouth out with water and ran a thin rag over her face. "As Salaam Alaikum, Malaya," Akeemah greeted Malaya at her cell door.

"Wa Alaikum Salaam." C-block consisted of four tiers. There was a top tier and a bottom tier on the left side of the unit, and a top and bottom tier on the right side of the unit. Each tier held fifteen cells, which made the C-block population one hundred and twenty if you counted two inmates per cell. Malaya couldn't believe how they had all of those women crammed in the small unit. C-block only had two TV rooms. One on each tier. The walls were dirty and it had so much black mold in the corners. The base was the unit which made Malaya feel sick to her stomach. It seemed that the women there were in no better shape than C-block. Most of the women were unkempt, hair was nappy, and their jumpsuits were wrinkled and dirty.

Stepping up to the food cart where the unit orderly was passing out food trays, Malaya and Akeemah got their trays and sat with Jada at an empty table. Jada was wolfing down her food like a mad woman. Malaya took one look at the lumpy oatmeal and half cooked boiled eggs and turned her nose up. "I can't eat this!" Malaya blurted out.

"Can I have it?" Jada asked.

"No," Akeemah said, eyeing Jada up and down. "Look, Malaya, you have to eat to keep your strength. The last thing you want to do in here is get sick. It's about survival now. We have to eat this until we can get some money to order canteen." Malaya knew Akeemah was right, she opened two sugar twin packs and dashed it on the oatmeal to drown out the nasty taste. Raising her head up from her tray, Malaya noticed all eyes were on her and Akeemah. One girl in particular eyed Malaya without breaking eye contact. The four girls crew looked on and shared whispers. "Jada, who them girls over there that's watching us with the cornrows?" Jada lifted her head from her tray.

"That's straight trouble. That's Dee-Dee and her girls. They run C-block. They are nothing but trouble, so stay away from them." Akeemah looked over to Dee-Dee and her crew. She could see that they were trouble.

"Malaya, from here on out, we got to stick together. I done seen them type of bitches before. They prey on the weak and those who are newcomers to the system. So know that you are a target for them and if you don't stand up to them, they're going to make your stay here rough by having you washing clothes and sucking pussy." Akeemah spoke like she was a true convict. Malaya wasn't a punk by a long shot, and Velli had taught her a few tricks on protecting herself. She knew that what Akeemah was saying was true, but she wondered could she trust Akeemah to have her back. Malaya knew she had to trust somebody. She looked over to Dee-Dee's staring eyes and repeated something she heard her husband Velli say to his friend E-Moe. "I make war with who makes war with you, and I make peace with who you make peace with." Jada just kept her head down in her tray, eating. Akeemah sensed that Jada was afraid of Dee-Dee. She just shook her head about the fact.

"Likewise, Malaya." Akeemah replied back to the oath Malaya just recited.

"When can we use the phones? I need to call my husband." Malaya asked, eyeing the phones that hung on the walls.

"8:00 o'clock when we come out for rec," Jada said. Akeemah just rolled her eyes at the frail woman. She didn't like Jada because she sensed she was a coward.

"I need to call Yah-Yah and see why he wasn't at court today and have him send me some money, so I can get the things I need to live in this rat hole." Akeemah looked around at her surroundings.

"Okay, ladies! Let's take it in!" the plump C.O. yelled, making it known that chow was over. "Turn all the trays in and step back to your cells." Malaya, Jada, and Akeemah returned their trays back to the food cart where they got them. Walking down on the bottom tier, Dee-Dee and her crew waited in front of Malaya and Jada's cell. Malaya stopped in front of her cell. Akeemah was right beside her.

"What's up?" Malaya asked Dee-Dee. Dee-Dee sized Malaya up.

"Girl, please," Dee-Dee said at Malaya, sending her friends into laughter. "Girl, come get these damn clothes. I need my shit washed and don't start getting brand new because this bitch is here," Dee-Dee said, looking past Malaya at Jada.

"Excuse me," Malaya said, stepping in Dee-Dee's face. "I'm not your bitch." Jada got in between Malaya and Dee-Dee.

"Give me the clothes. I'll wash them. That's what you want, right?" Jada asked, trying to defuse the situation.

"Yeah, wash this shit and tell your girl to watch herself," Dee-Dee replied, walking back to her cell.

"And I think it's best that you do the same because we ain't ducking no drama," Akeemah shot back. Dee-Dee just threw up her middle finger and walked in her cell.

Chapter 12

Velli's mind felt somewhat at peace after offering the morning congregation prayer at the Masjid. He knew that the Masjid was out his way from Wesley Chapel to Tampa, but he had fallen in love with that particular place of worship. It was something humbling about the Masjid. There were a few brothers that came to partake in the Morning Prayer. Shaking hands of a few brothers and giving up the Salaams, Velli made his way to the shoe rack, removed his Gucci slip-ons from the rack, and placed them on his feet. He had a few errands to run before the day was out, the most important one was to go see Malaya's lawyer. Velli needed to find out the best solution for Malaya. Velli knew that it was no way possible that Malaya could walk away from her situation as a free woman without doing some time. So, he and Mr. McCullough had to figure out how to get Malaya a lesser sentence. Walking out the Masjid into the parking lot, the sun was beginning to rise in the East part of the sky. "As Salaam Alaikum, Arki," someone greeted Velli from behind. Velli was so busy engrossed in his thoughts, he barely gave the brother a glance. "Wa Alaikum Salaam," Velli returned the greeting and kept it moving.

"It's been a long time, Velli. How is Malaya?" Velli became alert, hearing his wife's name. Spinning around, Velli faced Hakeem. Both men drew their weapons. Velli rested his 45 on the bridge of Hakeem's nose. Hakeem's large 357 cannon pushed into the flesh of Velli's right cheek.

"Malaya killed my wife. She took the only thing in the world that I love." Hakeem gripped his gun tighter.

"Your wife wasn't as special as you think she is. She violated and disrespected my family. She killed Ai'day, Anya's daughter. Keisha was fuck -"

"What is this," the frail man with the salt and pepper colored beard interrupted Velli and Hakeem's Mexican standoff. "What is this?" Iman Basil took another step closer to his Muslim brothers. "Muslim killing another Muslim. This is not the way of Islam. We're supposed to have love and help one another, but instead you two bring weapons to the house of Allah to harm one another." Iman Basil raised his voice, "You're not conducting yourselves like Muslims, but you're acting like deviants!" The words of their spiritual advisor softened the hearts of Velli and Hakeem. "This community has already lost Malaya and Keisha. Everyone has seen and heard the news, and the Islamic community is already talking. Please, don't give them anything else to discuss. Don't let Shayton claim you two in the hell fire. Put your guns away and go home." Iman Basil stood on the side of Velli and Hakeem and placed his small hand on each of their shoulders. "My brothers, please go home." Hakeem had so much love for Velli. He never had intentions to up his pistol on his old friend, but once he saw Velli his emotions got the best of him. Hakeem came to the Masjid to make final preparations for Keisha's janazah. When he saw Velli leaving the Masjid, he had so many questions for Velli. However, he knew that Velli was the type of man who wouldn't accept his apology for him pulling out his gun. There would be bloodshed between them in the future. Hakeem lowered his gun and backed away from Velli. "ALHAMDULILAH," (All praises to Allah) Basil whispered. Velli gritted his teeth still holding his 45. He was watching Hakeem's every move, but Iman Basil's words penetrated his ears and heart. Iman Basil stepped in front of Velli.

"Beloved, please put the gun away." Velli placed his gun in the small of his back as he watched Hakeem get into his car and pull out of the Masjid's parking lot.

***

Mango felt drained as he sat on the edge of the hotel bed. Splash and Peaches were some straight nymphos. They fucked Mango out of his sock. They sucked Mango dry to a no count. Mango never had two women that were so sexually aggressive. The more Mango jumped up and down on them, the more Splash and Peaches begged for more. When the two women ate Mango's ass out for his very first time, they had him speaking in tongue. Mango chuckled to himself as he looked back over his shoulder at Peaches and Splash sleeping. Just thinking about his sexual encounter with the two beauties, Mango's small member twitched. Mango was in D.C. for the last 24 hours waiting on Stone and his brother Mookie to show their faces, so he could find out what was going on with his shipment of drugs and money. Mango coming to the "W" hotel was his idea. He couldn't get comfortable fucking Splash and Peaches at Stone's house, so he brought them back to the "W" where he was staying. Mango knew that he was done having fun with Splash and Peaches. Now, it was time to find out what was going on with his product and money. Therefore, that would have to wait after his shower and breakfast. Mango reached over and grabbed the hotel's phone, ordered room service, and headed to the shower. Twenty minutes later, Mango walked out of the bathroom with a towel wrapped around him.

The light knock on the door, reminded Mango that he ordered room service. Answering the door, the bell boys pushed in three carts of food. It was enough food for a king. There were lumberjack pancakes, eggs, sausage links, beef and pork, and fluffy biscuits. The beverages were bottled water, orange juice and black coffee like Mango liked it along with a copy of the Washington Post. He gave the bell boys a tip and sent them on their way. Mango woke Splash and Peaches up to help consume the lovely breakfast. There was nothing greater to a man than to eat his breakfast with bare titties and pussy sitting in front of him. Mango smiled to himself as he watched the two women and their naked bodies crawl out of the bed. Pouring himself a cup of coffee and sitting down by the hotel window, Mango took a sip of the strong black coffee and opened the morning paper to see what was going on in the nation's capital. On the front page, two photos caught his attention. The caption read, "A notorious D.C. drug dealer and his brother found slain under a northeast bridge. Mango stared at the photo of Stone and Mookie. "Fuck!" Mango yelled, throwing the newspaper on the table, startling Splash and Peaches.

"What's wrong, Mango?" Splash asked, trying to understand what triggered Mango's outburst. Mango pointed to the paper. Splash saw her baby's father and Stone's picture, who was her secret lover on the front page of The Washington Post.

"Oh, shit!" Splash jumped up and ran over to her clothes that were draped over the arm of a chair and dressed quickly.

"Where are you going?" Mango demanded to know. Splash wasn't acting like she just lost a loved one.

"I-I got to go. Can you please call me a cab?" Splash asked, sliding into her 7 For All Mankind jeans.

"Here, take the keys to my car," Mango said, handing the keys to his 600 over to Splash. "I'll call you later to get my car." Peaches followed suit in getting dressed with Splash. Splash didn't even question why Mango was letting her use his Benz. She just took the keys and bounced. She was on a mission.

Chapter 13

2 days later

"You have a collect call from the Hillsborough County Detention Center, from Malaya." The jail recording blurred Malaya's name out. "To accept press '1' now." Velli pressed 1 to accept his wife's call. "As Salaam Alaikum, baby girl. How is my wife holding up?" Velli asked with excitement in his voice, trying to bring some joy into his wife's world.

"Wa Alaikum Salaam. I'm doing fine, babe. I just miss you like crazy. When are you coming to see your wife?"

"Real soon, baby, real soon. I'm just trying to tie up some loose ends, so when I do, it will be worth it." Malaya didn't like what she was hearing. She wanted to see her husband right then. She didn't care whether it was through a video monitor or not, but she didn't want to argue with Velli right then.

"Okay, baby, but I don't know how patient I can be," Malaya said, trying not to get upset.

"Just hold on, love. It will be worth it, but did you get the pictures that I sent along with the books I ordered from Amazon for you?"

"Yeah, Velli. I got the flicks and the books." Malaya giggled.

"What you laughing at, babe?" Velli questioned from the other end of the phone.

"I remember when you was locked up, I used to send you those sexy photos. Now you are sending me pictures of you wearing speedos with a hard dick." Malaya giggled again.

"Well, did it get that love box wet?"

"Oh! Yes, it did," Malaya said seductively, thinking about the photos that Velli sent her.

"Well, your husband did his job." Velli laughed through the phone. "Oh, I just put two grand on your account. I want you to buy everything that you want."

"I got the money, baby. Thank you so much."

"Malaya, listen baby." Seriousness came into Velli's voice.

"I'm listening, baby."

"You have to be careful of who you talk to in there. Some of them bitches is worse than niggas. They will get info about your case and use it to get out of jail, so it's best to keep your mouth closed. Do you hear me?"

"I definitely understand where you are coming from, baby."

"Mr. McCullough will come see you in a few days, so be ready for him when he comes."

"Okay, I will. How is my sister and brother?" Malaya didn't want to say Anya's and Damu's name over the phone.

"They are good. Just like me, they are worrying about you," Velli said with sadness in his voice.

"And how is Little Tiriq?" Malaya hadn't seen her nephew since the day Neva and Keisha kidnapped him.

"He's safe."

"You have one minute remaining." The recording notified Malaya and Velli that their call was ending.

"Baby, this phone is about to hang up. I will call you later," Malaya said, with tears in her eyes. She hated to get off the phone with Velli.

"I love you, baby. Stay strong in there." Velli tried to comfort his wife.

"I love you, too," Malaya said, hanging up the phone.

Malaya walked into the TV room where Akeemah was observing the movement in C-block.

"Salaam, Akeemah."

"Salaam, Malaya. What's wrong? You didn't get in touch with your husband?" Akeemah asked, seeing the sad look on Malaya's face.

"Yeah, girl. I got in contact with Velli. I just need to see him, that's all."

"Shit, at least you talked to him, and he put some money on your account so you can buy food and hygiene products. Shoot, I still haven't talked to Yah-Yah's ass yet," Akeemah said, eyeing Dee-Dee and her girls making cigarette transactions on the bottom tier. Malaya felt bad for complaining to Akeemah about not seeing Velli, when Akeemah hadn't spoken to or received any assistance from her man.

"Malaya, I need to make some money while I'm in here so I can take care of myself."

"Akeemah, what are you talking about?" Malaya looked confused.

"You heard me. I need to find out what these bitches in here is in demand of, and I need to find a way to supply it to them. That's how Dee-Dee is living better than everyone else in here."

"Hello, ladies," C.O. Hightower said as he walked into the TV room, interrupting Malaya and Akeemah's conversation.

"Hi," Malaya and Akeemah mumbled at the same time.

"I'm C.O. Hightower and C-block is my unit. If either of you have any problems with anyone or anything and I mean, anything just come to see me. We look out for each other on C-block, if you know what I mean," C.O. Hightower said, winking his eye at Malaya and Akeemah and licking his lips.

"Hmmm. We good," Akeemah said, catching on to what creep ass Hightower was suggesting. Akeemah grabbed Malaya's hand and exited the TV room. Walking down towards

Malaya's cell, they were approached by Dee-Dee and her flunkies.

"Let me tell you bitches something. You come in my house and disrespect me by talking to my man in my face."

"Your man? What the fuck you talking about," Akeemah asked, getting upset that Dee-Dee was coming with the bull-shit.

"Hightower, he's mine. Don't fuck with him." Dee-Dee stepped up to Akeemah exposing a tooth brush with a razor melted into the handle. Not wanting Akeemah to get hurt and both of them being outnumbered and without a weapon, Malaya grabbed Akeemah by the arm and pulled her away from Dee-Dee.

"Ok, Dee-Dee. You got that. We will respect your wishes," Malaya said, backing her up. Akeemah hesitated, but Malaya guided her out of harm's way.

"Don't trip, Akeemah. We going to handle her and her crew. She done fucked up, Akeemah. She fucked with the wrong one this time."

Chapter 14

Hakeem laid in Keisha's mother's spare bedroom. Yesterday was one of the worst days of his life. He did something that no man wished to ever do, and that's to bury his wife. A lot of people showed up. So many people loved Keisha. Hakeem still couldn't believe that she was gone, but now that she was gone, he must find out who were the two guys that were in the pictures that he found in Keisha's dresser. Hakeem reached and grabbed the two pictures that were on the nightstand next to the bed. He stared into the reddest nigga's eyes that he had ever seen. The guy was standing behind Keisha with his arms wrapped around her. Their body language proved that it was something between the two. Flipping to the next photo, Keisha was sitting on a dude's lap. The dude had cornrows in his head. His neck and wrist were draped in jewels. *"Who the fuck is this clown?"* Hakeem asked himself. A slight knock on the bedroom door broke Hakeem's thoughts. "Yeah," he answered. Iris walked in carrying a tray with a home cooked breakfast on it.

"Hey, sleepy head. I thought it would be nice of me to serve you breakfast in bed," Iris said with a smile. Hakeem sat up on the edge of the bed and planted his feet on the cold wooden floor. Iris stood in front of him wearing a small button down Polo shirt that barely covered her black lace panties. Standing 5'3 with sandy brown hair and a killer smile. Hakeem realized that he had been home almost a week, and he hadn't had any pussy yet. The creamy brown complexion of Iris' skin had his hormones on high alert. Iris' round melon sized breasts were perfect. Her rock hard nipples fought to be released from the confinement of her shirt. Her breasts begged to be touched. Iris' thick thighs and butta soft backside brought Hakeem to a full erection. Iris was a slight downgrade from Keisha, but nevertheless, she was well put together. Iris walked over to Hakeem to place the tray on his lap, so he could consume his breakfast. "Oops, I'm sorry. Did I do that?" Iris asked, pointing at the massive print that was standing up in Hakeem's boxers.

"It's been a while. I didn't mean no disrespect." Hakeem fumbled with his words.

Iris sat the tray on the floor next to the bed and sat next to Hakeem. She saw him yesterday at her Cousin Keisha's funeral and she knew she had to have him. That was the whole purpose of her spending the night at her Aunt Fatima's house. Iris knew she was wrong for going after Keisha's husband, but Keisha was dead and there was no need to let a brother like Hakeem slip by her. "There's no disrespect, handsome," Iris said, laying a hand on Hakeem's crotch. She began to stroke him through his boxers. The sensation sent shock waves through Hakeem's body. "How long has it been, Hakeem?"

"We can't do this. You are Keisha's cousin." Hakeem gasped for air through clenched teeth.

"I didn't ask you that. I asked you how long has it been." Iris eased her hand into Hakeem's boxers. She gripped Hakeem's throbbing dick.

"It's been 9 ½ years," Hakeem said, trying to control his breathing.

"Do you want this?" Iris questioned, pulling her panties to the side and placing two fingers in her wet love box.

"Yes, give it to me." Hakeem couldn't resist any longer. Iris pulled her fingers out her soaking wet pussy and placed them in Hakeem's mouth. Hakeem savagely sucked her juices from her fingers like a refugee that hadn't eaten in days. Tasting Iris in his mouth, Hakeem couldn't take it. He flipped her on her back effortlessly and ripped her black lace panties off, revealing her love box. Sliding his boxers below his waist and releasing his 8-inch manhood, his mushroom shaped head dripped with pre-cum. Iris took her thumb and made circular motions around the head of his love stick, lubricating it with his pre-cum. Hakeem bit down on his bottom lip, trying to control himself. Looking down in between Iris legs and seeing her smooth pussy lips sent him over the top. He pushed Iris back on the bed and spread her legs apart. Hakeem invaded her slurpy walls with his massive love stick. "OMG! Iris moaned out in ecstasy. "Oooh, Hakeem, you're so huge." Hakeem felt Iris' walls expand to their max, and he still pushed deeper, trying to get his full-length inside of her. Slightly pulling out, Hakeem saw his rod coated in Iris' wetness.

Iris grinded hard on Hakeem, trying to take him all in. Fitting like a glove, she was ready to take the pleasure and pain punishment that Hakeem was prepared to give her.

Hakeem picked up his pace. "This is what you want, huh?" Hakeem asked Iris as he stroked her harder.

"Yes! Give it to me. Give it to me nice and deep. I want all of it," Iris stuttered as she dug her nails into Hakeem's back. Hakeem felt his nuts drawing up, he couldn't hold back any longer. He exploded inside of Iris.

"Awwwwww!" Hakeem roared out. Iris stuck her panties into Hakeem's mouth to mute the noises he made. She didn't want to wake up her aunt that was just a few feet down the hall. Iris wrapped her legs around Hakeem and kissed his neck. Hakeem dumped nine years of pinned up sexual frustration into Iris. Pulling her panties out of his mouth, Hakeem felt a little guilty for having sex with his wife's cousin in her mother's house.

"I think that maybe we should go downstairs before Fatima wakes up and catches us," Hakeem said, pulling out of Iris' wetness and pulling his boxers up.

"Yeah, that sounds like a good idea." Iris stood up and fixed her shirt that barely concealed her goodies. "What's this?" Iris asked, picking the pictures up off the bed.

Hakeem hesitated. "Oh, those are some pictures that I found in Keisha's room. Do you know the dudes in the pictures with her?" Hakeem asked.

Iris looked at the pictures carefully. "Hmmmm yeah, I know them both. The red dude is Redz and the other dude with all the jewels on is Mike." Iris paused. "Hakeem, I don't mean to hurt you, but Keisha used to fuck with both of the dudes in the pictures. Redz got killed a few years ago and Mike got killed in front of Keisha's apartment the same night Keisha died."

Iris handed Hakeem the pictures back, gave him a kiss on the cheek, and exited the room, leaving him looking dumbfounded. Iris knew that Hakeem would be coming to her for more info on Keisha, and she had plenty of answers for him as long as he broke her off some of that good loving.

Chapter 15

"Oh, my God. Girl, look at all this damn money!" Peaches screamed.

"I'm going to Paris for sure, and I don't need Stone's dead ass to take me. I got all this money with all them dead presidents on them," Splash said, picking up a stack of money off the bed and thumbing through it. "I thought that locksmith would never get into that floor safe. It took him two hours to blow torch the hinges off of it."

"The reason it took him so long was because he couldn't take his eyes off your phat ass in them thongs," Peaches said, smacking Splash on the ass and laughing. "How much is there?" Peaches asked.

"I don't know, but Stone's been stashing money here for the last few months. He's the one who had the floor safe put in. It's probably three hundred thousand or more. Let's count it and see, then after we finish, we can fuck on it." Splash laughed.

"No more fucking and sucking dicks to get ahead in the game. We are now paid in full," Splash stated, sitting on the bed and counting the money.

"Splash, it's going to take us all day to count this damn money," Peaches replied, picking up a fist full of money and helping Splash count it.

"Peaches, do you still be fucking with Wayne from Simple City?"

"Yeah, why?" Peaches asked looking at the road dawg crazy.

"Because I know where Stone got his coke stashed."

"What that got to do with Wayne?" Peaches asked, still confused as to why Splash asked about Wayne.

"I want to sell Wayne a piece of Stone's stash for the low."

"Oh, I got cha. I understand. Hold up. Splash, is this the same stash that Mango is looking for?" Peaches inquired.

"Yep," Splash said with a smile on her face.

"You knew where the drugs were the whole time?" Peaches asked, looking wide-eyed.

"Hell yeah, and I wasn't going to tell Mango I knew where his stash was at," Splash admitted rolling her eyes. "Stone had rented a storage space out in Hyattsville, MD. The storage space is in my name. Stone thought he had the only key, but the storage company provides you with two sets of keys. I gave one to Stone and didn't let him know that I had a spare key to the storage unit. I went out there by myself just to see what Stone was using the unit for. You know a bitch had to be nosy," Splash said smiling. "The storage space was filled with bricks." Peaches just shook her head, listening to her crime partner tell her story of how she was a sneaky bitch and how she got paid for being that sneaky bitch.

"Damn, Splash, you are too damn shady for me." Peaches laughed.

"Shit, you say what you want to, but I got to look out for me. Nobody is going to look out for you but you, and the quicker you learn that, the quicker you will start to see shit a whole lot different." Splash made eye contact with Peaches.

"What are you going to do about Mookie?"

"What about him?" Splash asked, looking at Peaches with her face twisted.

"Aren't you going to his funeral and pay your respects?"

"Respects? Mookie don't respect me! He didn't care about me when he was fucking all them bitches when I was pregnant. Why would I give a fuck about a nigga that gave me an STD while I was pregnant with his son." Splash was becoming emotional. Peaches didn't know what to say. If Mookie would have taken her through the things he took Splash through, she'd be singing that same tune. Therefore, she felt where Splash was coming from. However, what was really on Peaches' mind was how much money Splash was going to give her.

"Girl, don't even trip off Mookie. If you say, fuck him then fuck him. I'm not going to the funeral either. So, let's count this money and make a plan to spend it," Peaches said, smiling at Splash.

***

Mango puffed on his cigar as he sat in front of Splash's crib in a navy-blue Buick, waiting on his hired hand to come back from Splash's house. The GPS system that Mango had on his 600 Benz came in handy. He called OnStar and told them that he had too many drinks at a party and forgot where he parked his car. OnStar gave Mango the precise location of where his car was parked. The way Splash was acting when she found out that her baby's father and lover was murdered, let Mango know that she had some shit with her and that he needed to know what she knew. So, he gave her his Benz to use so he could track her movements. "They're in their house counting money," Peppay said, climbing behind the wheel of the Buick and closing the door.

"What else you see, Peppay?"

"We was right. That locksmith came to open the safe, and they are counting up the money now."

"Did you see the coke?" Mango asked.

"No coke, just green backs."

"Okay, Amigo! Let's go get my money."

***

Splash and Peaches were viciously counting up the money that was spread across the bed. "Damn, this is a lot of money to be counting by hand, Splash."

"I know, Peaches. We are going to need some money counting machines. My hand is starting to cramp up," Splash complained.

"Splash, be honest with me. How much money are you going to give me? I mean, a bitch is broke. I'm going to need a few dollars to get right." Knock, Knock. The knock at the door silenced Peaches' inquiry on her cut of the money.

"Who the fuck is that?" Splash asked, tip-toeing to the front door of her three bedroom home. Looking through the peephole and seeing Mango starting back at her made her heart fall to her stomach. "What the fuck is going on in here? How in the hell does he know where I live at?" Splash turned around and headed back to the bedroom. "Girl, help me put this money away. Mango's at the door." Splash and Peaches covered the money up with the blanket that was folded at the foot of the bed. Splash threw on some jeans and a Washington Redskins football jersey that belonged to Stone. She placed one of the guns that was inside the floor safe in the small of her back. "Come on, Peaches. Let's go see what this mutha-fucka wants."

"Hey, Mango," Splash said, trying to act surprised to see him.

"Hello, Splash," Mango said, stepping into the house un-invited, following behind Peppay. Splash didn't see Peppay when she first looked through the peephole earlier. *"He must have been standing on the side of the door frame,"* Splash thought to herself.

"Oh, you must be here to pick up your car. Let me go get the keys." Splash went to the bedroom and retrieved Mango's car keys off the dresser. Splash entered back into the living room. She stopped dead in her tracks. Peppay stood behind Peaches with a handful of weave and a nine-inch Rambo-styled knife aimed at Peaches' throat. Splash's heart thumped hard in her chest.

"Give me the keys," Mango cool and calmly said to Splash. Splash tossed the keys to Mango. He caught them in mid-air. "Let me get that money too that you got in the back room."

"How did he know about the money?" Splash thought to herself. Splash led the way to the money, with Mango and his goon on her heels. Splash pulled the blanket back off the bed and piles of big faces stared back at Mango. "Empty them pillow cases and fill them with the money," Mango instructed while standing next to Peppay while he still held Peaches hostage at knife point. "Let the bitch go, Peppay, so she can help Splash fill them pillow cases up." Peaches flew over to the bed and helped Splash with stuffing money into the pillow cases. "Where is the coke?" Mango asked. The wheels in Splash's head started to turn.

"You talking about the stash that has the red Texas star stamp on its package?"

"Yeah, where's my shit?" Mango asked, getting mad, then realizing Splash had his product the whole time.

"It's not here, but I'll take you to it if you let us live," Splash said, still stuffing money in the pillow cases.

"I'm not going to hurt you, love. I just want what's mine."

"You lying, bitch!" Splash yelled as she reached in the small of her back, pulled out a 9 mm Ruger, and fired a shot, hitting Peppay in the shoulder.

Mango was caught off guard. Mango cowardly hid behind the bedroom door. "Listen, Splash, just put the gun down. We can talk about this. I wasn't going to hurt you." Mango stumbled over his words.

"We don't have shit to talk about," Splash said, still pointing the gun at Mango.

"Peaches, grab the money and let's go," Splash ordered Mango to the other side of the room and made him lay down on the floor. "If your fat ass comes out this house before I'm gone, I'll kill your fucking ass!" Splash screamed at Mango. Peppay moaned in pain on the floor as he held his shoulder. Peaches ran over and kicked him in the face. "You bitch ass, nigga. That's for putting that knife to my throat."

"Come on. Let's go, Peaches!" Splash yelled. Peaches grabbed the pillowcases and exited the room. Just to put a little fear in Mango, Splash fired two shots by Mango's head. BOOM! BOOM! "You come out; you die." Splash vanished out of the house behind Peaches.

Chapter 16

Malaya walked in the small legal visiting room. Seeing her lawyer made her feel that she was going to be okay. Mr. McCullough sat behind the small square table, reading over some papers. "Hello, Mrs. Williams," Mr. McCullough said, jumping to his feet and extending his hand.

"Hi, Mr. McCullough." Malaya accepted his hand.

"How are they treating you in here?"

"I really understand what Dorothy on The Wizard of Oz meant when she said, there's no place like home."

"Well, I'm here to see if I can get you home," Mr. McCullough stated with confidence.

"Do you think that's possible with all the incriminating evidence they have against me?" Malaya put her head down and stared at her small hands.

"Anything is possible. Have you lost your faith in me already? Remember, I freed your husband when no one else could." Malaya thought back to the time when all odds were against her husband and when it seemed like nothing in the world could have freed Velli from prison. Then Mr. McCullough came along and did the unthinkable and brought Velli home to her. It cost a hefty fee, but it was worth it.

"Yes, I have faith that Allah will help you be victorious." Malaya replied, looking Mr. McCullough in his eyes.

"With that said, tell me what happened from the beginning. I mean everything from the time of the kidnapping up to the moment that you killed Keisha." Malaya was shocked that her lawyer knew about Tiriq's kidnapping. Mr. McCullough sensed that Malaya was uncomfortable about conveying to him the story of the kidnapping. "Don't worry, Malaya. Velli told me everything, but I need to hear it from you."

***

Akeemah ferociously worked her lips and jaw muscles up and down on C.O. Hightower's love stick. The more that she bobbed her head back and forth, Hightower savagely fucked her mouth like it was a virgin. Tears fell from Akeemah's eyes. She hated herself for stooping so low, but she needed some means to take care of herself while she was in jail. She couldn't understand why Yah-Yah abandoned her after all that she had done for him. Akeemah was a survivor, and she was determined to survive. Therefore, when C.O. Hightower made a proposition for her to take C-block's trash out for a $100 and a carton of Newport, it motivated her. Now she was in the trash room down the hall from C-block tongue kissing his love muscle. The Newport alone were worth $50 a pack. That would put $500 in her account if things went well. "Oh, right there. I'm about to cum." Hightower grabbed the back of Akeemah's head and pumped harder in and out of her mouth. Hightower shot a thick load in her mouth. Akeemah slid her mouth off Hightower's manhood. Her mouth was loaded with his juices. She was preparing to spit the nut in the corner of the trash room, but Hightower stopped her. "You betta not! You want every dime of your money, and I want you to swallow every drop of me," Hightower said with a stern face. Akeemah felt like throwing up, but she held her breath and swallowed hard. "Good, girl," Hightower said, smiling ear to ear and opening one of the trash bags that Akeemah just carried to the trash room and pulled out a carton of Newport 100s. Akeemah opened the carton, stuffed the cigarettes down her panties and into her bra, and fixed her clothes.

"Let's go," Akeemah said with her head down. Hightower grabbed her face. "Keep your mouth shut about this and the next time, I'll let you get some of this dick."

***

Malaya felt good coming back from seeing her lawyer. She walked down to Akeemah's cell to convey her conversation that she had with her lawyer. Akeemah was the only person that she could talk to and trust. Reaching Akeemah's cell, Malaya looked in and to her surprise, Akeemah wasn't in there. *"Where could she be?"* Malaya thought to herself. Malaya noticed that Dee-Dee and her girls were mean grilling her. Malaya felt they may try to jump her because Akeemah was gone somewhere. Malaya quickly eased in her cell and dug in the hole of her mattress, where she stashed an old toothbrush with three razors melted into the handle of it. Malaya and Akeemah made two of the weapons the same day that Dee-Dee pulled the razor on them. Malaya came back on the tier to let Dee-Dee know she wasn't scared. Just then, the sally port opened and Akeemah stepped through it with C.O. Hightower right behind her. Akeemah made her way to her cell, while Hightower stopped and talked to a group of inmates that were playing spades in the dayroom. Malaya could tell that something was wrong by how Akeemah was looking. Akeemah couldn't make eye contact with Malaya. She just walked right pass Malaya as if she wasn't there. Dee-Dee looked at Akeemah like she could just kill her. Malaya followed Akeema to her cell. "Girl, what's going on with you?" Akeemah's eyes misted over as she made eye contact with Malaya for the first time.

"I had to do what I had to do." Akeemah started unloading the cigarettes onto her bunk.

"Akeemah, what are you talking about?" Malaya asked, looking puzzled. Akeemah just looked at Malaya with a blank stare, then it hit Malaya like a Mike Tyson punch. "You fucked Hightower for some cigarettes?" Malaya asked, looking crazy at Akeemah like she'd lost her damn mind.

"These cigarettes are worth $500, and he's going to put $100 in my account, so I can buy the things I need in here." Malaya became furious.

"What the fuck type of games you on, Akeemah?"

"I got to fend for mine, sister."

"I wish you would have told me that you was going to do some dumb shit like that before I had my husband to put a $1,000 dollars on your account." Akeemah was looking crazy after hearing this.

"Why would you do that?" Akeemah asked.

"I told my lawyer to give my husband your name and number and to send you the money. I got your info from your arm band."

"But why?" Akeemah asked.

"Because we are Muslim and Muslims are supposed to look out for one another," Malaya said with sincerity.

"I'm sorry. I didn't know."

"Sister, don't be sorry. Just don't do it again, and plus I got a way to get cigarettes without having to fuck Hightower. Save that shit for Dee-Dee and them other bitches."

"But how are we going to get cigarettes?" Akeemah asked, looking confused.

"I got this," Malaya said, pulling out her iPhone.

Chapter 17

A week later...

Malaya laid in her bed talking to Velli on her smartphone. It had been the third time today that she and Velli had phone sex through FaceTime. Seeing Velli stroke his massive cock on screen, did something to Malaya, but seeing the live ejaculation was too much for Malaya. The more that she saw Velli unload his love juices onto the screen, the more Malaya craved for him. "Damn, baby. Being in there got you so nasty." Velli laughed.

"I know right, baby," Malaya said, cleaning her sinful juice stained fingers.

"Remember when I was doing time in Coleman Pen? We used to have the steamy phone sex sessions early in the morning."

"Do I remember? They were the best. It's strange how the roles have changed, though. Back then, you were doing time for murder, and now I'm doing a bid for murder," Malaya said sadly.

Velli heard the sadness in his wife's voice. "Yeah, I know, baby. I'm going to do everything in my power to make sure that you don't have to do any time," Velli assured his wife, trying to bring Malaya some comfort.

"Inshallah," (if God willing) Malaya replied.

"Baby, I miss you. We are going to get through this just like everything else."

"I miss you too, Velli." Malaya was on the verge of tears. She changed the subject. "Thank you for sending that money, baby."

"It's no problem, baby. A sister of yours is definitely a sister of mine. But what type of sister is Akeemah?"

"A sister that's trying to find her way back to Islam."

"Just like Keisha was," Velli mistakenly said to Malaya.

"Hell, NO! She's much different from Keisha."

"Okay, baby. Just be careful."

"Hey, baby. Let me go. I got to put this phone on the charger and plus I told Akeemah she could call her man to see what's going on with him."

"Okay, baby. I love you."

"I love you too, hubby." Malaya disconnected the call. Malaya walked over to the cell door and removed the piece of cardboard that was in her window to prevent anyone from looking in her cell while she was using the phone or the restroom. As soon as Akeemah saw Malaya remove the cardboard from out the cell door window, she came into the cell. "You finish getting your freak on," Akeemah said, smiling.

"Yup." Malaya playfully batted her eyes.

"It's about time. You had me watching out for about twenty-five minutes. I thought you was never going to bust your nut."

"Whatever, girl." Both of them broke out in laughter. "Here. Go ahead and call Yah-Yah and see if you can get a hold of him," Malaya said, handing Akeemah the phone. Akeemah had been trying to catch up with Yah-Yah ever since Malaya had gotten the phone from her lawyer, but for some reason Yah-Yah wasn't answering his phone. Akeemah dialed Yah-Yah's number with nervous hands. Malaya stood at the door watching out for any C.O.'s or nosy inmates. Yah-Yah's phone began to ring. He picked up on the third ring. Akeemah called out his name.

"Yah-Yah!"

"Yeah! Who the fuck is this?" Yah-Yah said with an attitude.

"It's me. Akeemah." A small silence came over the phone. "Hello," Akeemah asked again, trying to make sure that Yah-Yah was still on the phone.

"Yeah, I'm here."

"What's going on with you, Yah-Yah. I been calling you. Why you haven't been answering your phone?"

"I been busy ... My bad."

"You been busy? What type of fuck shit is that?" Akeemah said with hurt feelings.

"Baby, are you hungry?" Akeemah heard a woman's voice ask in the background through the phone.

"Who the fuck is that, Yah-Yah?"

"Nobody."

"I'm sitting in this rat hole because of you, and you are out there playing house with some bitch. You could have at least respected me enough to put some money in my account."

"I'm not playing house, Akeemah."

"Then who's that talking in the background?" Yah-Yah ignored Akeemah's question.

"How are you calling me, anyway?" Yah-Yah inquired.

"Don't worry about that. Is she the reason why you haven't showed up for my court dates, or why you haven't been here to see me?" Akeemah began to cry.

"What the fuck you want me to do, Akeemah? You are the one locked up, not me." Yah-Yah was losing his cool and getting upset at all the hard questions that Akeemah shot at him.

"That was your gun they found in my car, not mine."

"Look, Akeemah. Sometimes shit just happens."

"Okay, remember them same words, muthafucka! Because what goes around comes around, bitch!" Akeemah shouted into the phone and disconnected the call. Handing the phone back to Malaya, Malaya felt sorry for Akeemah. She wrapped her arms around Akeemah and let her cry her eyes out.

Chapter 18

Mango was in a foul mood as he sat in the backseat of his cocaine white 600 Benz. Heading towards Velli's house, he was furious that he allowed Splash to get away from him, but what was running his blood pressure high was that he received a phone call from one of his contacts in South Beach, Florida that Mike was gunned down in Tampa. Mango went online to confirm the information. The online newspaper read: Michael Coleman was gunned down in front of his ex-girlfriend Keisha Timmons' apartment. There were also 3 other bodies found inside Mrs. Timmons' apartment. Rico Wallo, Andrew Smith, and Neva Timmons were shot to death inside of Mrs. Timmons' apartment. Keisha Timmons was gunned down by suspect Malaya Williams. Mango couldn't believe his eyes. He had past history with Keisha from a few years ago. She used to traffic cocaine back and forth from Texas to Florida for Mike. During her stay in Texas, she and Mango established a pay and play relationship. He'd give her a few grand, and Keisha would spread her legs for him in any and every way that Mango pleased. Mango was pissed at what he had read, he knew now that Velli had something to do with Mike's murder if his wife Malaya was sitting in jail for Keisha's murder. Mango rode in silence, thinking about the situation he was in. With Mike and Stone being dead, moving product for the Sicaro Cartel back home in Mexico was going to be a problem. His numbers in moving the product were surely going to drop, and the Sicaro's were definitely going to take notice and ask why. He couldn't let the Sicaro's know that he'd been dealing with the blacks. Mango had to fix this and fix it fast. Mango called a meeting with Velli and his brother Damu. He wanted to know how much they knew and how much info they would give him about Mike's death. But, most importantly, he had to build his numbers back up.

***

Velli checked his watch as he heard the doorbell chime. *"Damn. Damu and Biggz are early,"* Velli thought to himself. Wicket barked viciously at the front door. "Be easy, Wicket," Velli commanded, bringing him to a humble sitting position. Velli looked through the peephole and saw Yvette standing on the other side of the door. It made Velli smile.

"What's up, Yvette?" Velli said, opening the door.

"Hey, Velli." Yvette batted her golden brown eyes at Velli. I came to bring you some food and to check up on you. I noticed that you haven't been coming to the coffee and tea house ever since Malaya got locked up."

"I know. Things been rough for me since Malaya's been gone," Velli said with sadness in his voice. "But that's nice of you to bring a brother something to eat and to check on me. Come on in." Velli opened the door wider, letting Yvette in the house.

"I have chicken and dirty rice with buttermilk rolls." Yvette took a survey of the house as she walked in.

"That sounds nice. The kitchen is this way." Velli led his guest to the kitchen. Yvette was 5'5 with small breasts and a perfect round ass. She favored Erykah Badu, but just a little lighter in the skin complexion. She had a killer smile to go along with her round beautiful face, but her golden dreads highlighted her beauty. Yvette was the wife of Velli, the comrade Chief. To help with Chief's struggle of being incarcerated, Velli went into business with Yvette at Felicitous Coffee House in North Tampa. The business was doing pretty good.

"I just love this house," Yvette said, admiring Velli's house.

"Yeah, Malaya does too," Velli said, getting a plate out of the cabinet over the sink. "How is Chief doing?" Yvette let out a deep breath.

"He is fine. He's still working on the case."

"What is the lawyer talking about?" Velli questioned, scooping the rice out of the Tupperware bowl and placing it on his plate.

"He's not talking about much, just saying everything is a process, and we have to be patient."

"Well, look. Tell Chief to never stop fighting and anything that I can do to help, just holla at me, and he got it."

"I will let him know." Velli placed the chicken and rice in the microwave and set the timer for 2 ½ minutes. Yvette watched Velli's every move from the very first time Chief had her meet Velli about investing some money into her coffee house. Yvette admired Velli, but she kept her distance because Velli was married. Now that Malaya was away fighting murder charges, Yvette was on some R-Kelly down low shit. She loved the hell out of Chief, but a woman gets lonely at times, and she definitely had her needs that needed to be filled. She figured she'd see if she could have something with Velli and if Malaya somehow got out of jail soon, she'd just fade into the shadows like nothing ever happened.

"How is the business?" Velli asked, breaking Yvette's thoughts.

"It's doing great thanks to you." Yvette smiled hard at Velli. The microwave beeped, letting Velli know that his food was ready. Velli retrieved the food from the microwave and placed it on the island in the middle of the kitchen.

"Damn, Yvette. This is the bomb, good looking out," Velli said, sampling the rice.

"Let me get you something to drink." Yvette made her way over to the fridge, grabbed Velli a coke, and handed it to him. Their hands touched, and heat waves shot down between Yvette's thighs, causing her panties to become soaked. "Next time, I'm going to make you my meatloaf and apple pie. Oh, you got to taste my apple pie. I haven't had a man to deny it yet," Yvette said with sweetness in her voice and placed her hand on the small of Velli's back.

"Who the fuck is this bitch!" Anya yelled, standing in the kitchen's doorway. Anya's sudden presence caught Velli off guard and made Yvette snatch her hand from the small of Velli's back, giving the impression to Anya that something was going on in her sister's house.

"Oh. Hey, sis," Velli said, trying to play it cool.

"Hey sis, my ass. Bitch, what's your name?" Anya directed her attention to Yvette.

"Oh, I'm Yvette, and I'm not a bitch." Yvette got offended by Anya's approach.

"Velli, what's she doing here?" Anya asked, walking over to Velli.

"She just brought me something to eat and to check up on me."

"Well, I'm here to check up on you. Ms. Yvette, you can leave now. My sister hasn't been in jail for two months, and you already got a woman in her house," Anya scolded Velli.

"Anya, chill out. This is my business partner."

"I don't give a fuck! Yvette, let's go!" Yvette followed Anya to the front door. Anya held the door open for her. "Let me ask you something, Yvette? Does my sister know you?"

"I don't think so." Yvette looked puzzled.

"Okay, good, then I can say this and mean it. The next time I catch you in my sister's house with her husband, I'm beating the brakes off you." Yvette stared Anya in the eyes and smirked. Yvette walked out the front door, leaving Anya to stare holes in her back.

Chapter 19

Hakeem had so many thoughts running through his mind after reading the newspaper and finding out his Muslim brother, Muhammad Stevenson Wallo was killed at his wife Keisha's apartment. *"What was he doing there? Why Keisha never mentioned she was in contact with Steve? Were they lovers?"* All types of thoughts danced through Hakeem's head. He needed answers to his questions. Through digging around, he knew that his wife Keisha had dealt with a whole lot of men while he was away. Despite the fact that Hakeem knew this, he still had the urge to get revenge for Keisha's death. "Aye, Iris!" Hakeem called out from the next room. Lately, he had grown somewhat fond of Iris. She took away his pain when he was hurting, he'd been staying with her ever since their sexual encounter.

"Yeah, Bae."

"Let me holla at you for a minute."

Iris came from out of the back room of her two bedroom apartment. "Yeah, Bae. What's up?" Iris said, sitting on Hakeem's lap.

"You ever seen this dude before?" Hakeem asked, showing her Steve's picture in the newspaper. Iris looked at the picture as if she was going to confirm that she didn't recognize the man Hakeem was asking her about.

"Oh yeah, I met him once. Keisha told me he had just come home from prison or something like that."

"Do you know what he was doing at Keisha's house?"

"Come on, Hakeem. Let it go. Keisha is gone. You can't keep investigating Keisha's murder like you are the police. You have to move on."

"I didn't ask you for all of that. I asked you why he was at my wife's house."

Iris just looked at Hakeem with a stupid expression on her face.

"They were lovers," Iris said, getting off his lap and heading towards the back of the apartment, leaving Hakeem's heart bleeding from the wound she just caused him.

Hakeem had to find out what was going on. The only person he felt that could give him the answers he needed was Velli.

***

Velli intensely watched Mango as he sat on the other side of the living room. He felt thankful that Damu invited his right hand man Biggz to sit in on the meeting. Mango brought one of his shooters with him, and that fact alone made Velli a little nervous. Mango's shooter stayed standing while his boss sat and talked. Biggz did the same, keeping an eagle's eye on Mango and his bodyguard. There definitely was some type of tension in the room. Damu stood behind the bar, nursing a drink in one hand and a Mack 11 in the other.

"How's business, Velli?" Mango asked while puffing on his cigar.

"All is well. Everyone is eating on my team. We have no complaints. The money that's right there at your feet should prove to you that everything is everything," Velli said, acknowledging the money that laid in the duffle bag at Mango's feet.

"I see that the money flow has picked up in a major way in D.C., my friend. You must have eliminated the competition."

"You know how I do. You eat with us, or you don't eat at all. If there's ratting, then you cut the heads off them bitches and leave them in the streets to rot." Velli made straight eye contact with Mango.

It seemed like the tension in the room grew thicker. Mango was tired of playing games with Velli. "Why you kill Mike?"

"Why was you supplying Stone when you was supposed to be supplying me?" Velli answered Mango's question with a question.

"I can supply who the fuck I want to supply, amigo. It's just business."

Mango shifted his weight in his chair. Damu gripped his gun tighter. "Now, why you kill Mike?"

"I didn't kill Mike. Your man was in the wrong place at the wrong time."

"Do you know how much fucking money I'm losing because of Mike being dead?"

"So you knew Mike was alive all that time?" Velli questioned Mango.

"Like I said, Velli. It was all in the name of business. I wasn't going to let the feud between you and Mike come between my money." Velli clenched his jaw tight. He wanted to whip his gun off his waist and empty the clip in Mango's fat ass. However, he didn't know who Mango told that he was coming there.

"I can respect that. It was all in the name of business and Stone was just business too, right? That rat bitch sent me away for almost ten years. Was supplying a rat just part of business?" Velli asked.

"Listen, Stone is dead and Mike is dead. I need to find a way to move more product," Mango said, standing ignoring Velli's question. "I'm going to double your shipment to D.C., handle that and I will be in touch." Mango signaled for his bodyguard to grab the duffle bag off the floor. Mango exited Velli's house with his bodyguard on his heels.

"Velli, let me kill both of them fools," Damu said, watching Mango and his escort from the porch.

"As soon as we get a handle on Malaya's situation, then we moving on. Don't even trip, bruh. We got him," Velli said with confidence.

Chapter 20

Malaya and Akeemah had been living the county jail life as ballers. For the last two months, there was nothing the two wanted and couldn't get their hands on. They had the perfect system. Malaya had her husband, Velli, to throw a few extra dollars to Mr. McCullough. Every week, like clockwork, Mr. McCullough came through and dropped a package off. Velli wouldn't agree on sending any drugs into the jail, but Malaya and Akeemah had an unlimited supply of cigarettes and finger vibrators for those who liked to have a little fun while on lock down. A couple of Dee-Dee's so-called friends went behind Dee-Dee's back and brought a few packs of Newports from Malaya and Akeemah.

"Salaam, (peace) Malaya," Akeemah said, as she entered Malaya's cell.

"Salaam, sis," Malaya said, looking up from the table full of food. Malaya was making a nacho dish for her, Akeemah, and Jada. They had been eating good for weeks. Every week, Malaya and Akeemah would speed the max allowed for them to spend at commissary, which was $75. They ordered everything, which was corn chips, soups, beef salami, tuna, honeybuns, cookies, and hygiene products. Everything that one could think of, Hillsborough County sold it on the commissary. "Damn, the food looks good and smells even better," Akeemah said, eyeing the nacho bowl.

"Wait until you taste it. Did you charge the phone back up?" Malaya asked.

"Yeah, I did. Here." Akeemah handed the IPhone to Malaya and watched her stash it in her mattress along with the charger. They had to sneak in the mop closet in the back of the tier to charge the phone up. The mop closet had the only plug in the unit that was out of the eyesight of the officers and the snitches. During that time while the phone was being charged, one would sit in front of the mop closet washing clothes as a decoy until the phone was charged back up and ready to be used again.

"Girl, let's make these bitches mad and go eat our food in the day room in front of them broke ass bitches," Akeemah boasted.

"Naw, Akeemah. We are not here to make enemies. We're doing big things, so we got to keep a low profile. We are making a $1,000 dollars a piece every week. So, why cause trouble for ourselves?"

The money was peanuts to Malaya, but Akeemah didn't know that.

"Damn, sis. You are always thinking two steps ahead of the game."

"That's the way that it has to be, and you know that Dee-Dee and her girls are going to try us soon, right? But when they do, I want to smash their asses," Malaya said with a serious face. Akeemah nodded her head in agreement.

"Who is the other bowl of nachos for?" Akeemah inquired. Malaya hesitated.

"Oh, that's for Jada."

"Jada! That bitch don't deserve nothing to eat. Tell her to let Dee-Dee feed her, since she be washing that dirty bitch's socks and drawers."

Malaya sighed. "Akeemah we are Muslims. We don't treat people like that. Why not give her something to eat? At the end of the day, she is just trying to survive, just like us."

"I don't care, Malaya. She don't deserve shit," Akeemah said, getting frustrated at Malaya.

"Listen, Akeemah. Remember the story about the prostitute that took her leather shoe off and filled it up with water to give a thirsty dog a drink of water? That gesture alone was favored by Allah and granted paradise. Do you think that woman deserves it?" Malaya asked. Akeemah was at a loss for words.

"Hey, you two," Jada said, walking into the cell with a handful of clothes. Akeemah rolled her eyes.

"Girl, them clothes stink like hell. Who clothes are those?" Akeemah asked, covering her nose and mouth up with her hand.

"Dee-Dee and her cellmate Tiffany."

"You still washing them dumb bitches clothes!" Akeemah screamed.

"This is how I fend for myself," Jada said with her head down.

Malaya couldn't take it anymore. "Listen, Jada. From now on, you work for me and nobody else. I'm going to pay you a $100 every two weeks to not wash nobody's clothes on C-block. From now on, you are officially on cook duty. You'll cook all the meals for me and Akeemah. And every time that me and Akeemah eat, you eat. Now go take them clothes back to Dee-Dee." Jada shot out the cell with Dee-Dee and Tiffany's clothes with lightning speed.

"You know that it's on and popping, right?" Akeemah asked. "Dee-Dee and them bitches are going to be coming."

"I already got it," Akeemah said, pulling the box cutter out that was sent in by Velli. Malaya grabbed hers out of her shoe and they both exited the cell. Jada almost knocked Malaya down because she moved fast to get back to warn Malaya and Akeemah that Dee-Dee and her crew were coming. When Malaya saw the gang of hardcore bitches coming her way, she wished her sister, Anya, was beside her to go head up with that group of bitches.

"You got something that you want to say to me?" Dee-Dee loudly asked. Malaya just palmed her razor, waiting for the right move. Akeemah already had her razor out. Jada ducked off into the cell.

"Make it do what it do," Akeemah said, going into her attack stance. The four girls surrounded her and Malaya.

"Jada is my flunky. She's washing my shit until I leave this bitch," Dee-Dee said, staring Malaya down and stopping in her tracks once she saw Malaya and Akeemah's blades.

"Jada ain't doing shit for you and your crew no more," Malaya said, holding her ground.

"Yeah, we will see about that." Dee-Dee pulled her own razor out of her waistband and took a step closer with the razor held out.

"Hold the fuck up!" a heavy set female C.O. yelled. As she ran down onto the tier, all of the women cuffed their razors. "Is it a problem?" the C.O. asked, eyeing every last one of the women. "Because I will send all your asses to the fucking hole if you all start some shit on C-block." The C.O. scolded the group.

"Nah, we don't have a problem," Dee-Dee said, staring at Malaya.

"Well, let's break this huddle up then," the C.O. ordered. Dee-Dee walked by Malaya and mumbled, "It's on, bitch."

"Ready when you are," Malaya mumbled back and walked down towards the day room with Akeemah. Jada let out a deep breath as she peeped out the door of her cell with her hand tightly gripped around the handle of the ice pick.

Chapter 21

"How are you holding up in there, sis?" Anya asked as she stared at Malaya on the screen of her IPhone.

"I'm holding on, Anya. I just miss my husband and my family." Hearing Malaya mention her husband, Anya wondered was it wise to tell her about Velli having that Yvette chic all up in her house.

"We miss you, too. Malaya, I know that I haven't been to see you yet, but until I find out what's up with your situation, I have to keep my distance just in case they find out something that will link me and Damu to the murders at Keisha's apartment."

"I understand, girl. I wouldn't have it no other way." Malaya adjusted the phone in her hand. "But thanks for the pictures, books, and magazines. I tell you, between you and Velli I got enough books and shit to start a small library." Anya laughed at Malaya's joke.

"We do that because we love you, and we don't want your mind running wild in there." Anya couldn't take it any longer, she had to ask her sister. "Malaya, why did you do it?" Malaya looked confused for a second. She didn't know what Anya was talking about, then it hit her. Malaya lowered her head.

"I was so tired of her hurting the people that I loved. She was like a ghost that kept coming back to haunt us. I couldn't stand it anymore, so I made the sacrifice. That's why I killed Keisha."

"But I should have made that sacrifice. She killed my daughter. She is the one who kidnapped my son." Anya began to cry. "I'm sure she was behind my husband, Damu getting shot. I needed to make that sacrifice. I should be sitting in there, not you, Malaya. I miss you so much." Anya broke down, releasing a river full of tears. Malaya cried with her sister.

"Anya, I got to go. It's about time for the C.O.'s to make their rounds." This wasn't true. Akeemah was right outside the cell door, keeping watch.

"Okay, sis," Anya said, wiping her eyes.

"Give Damu my Salaams and kiss Tiriq for me."

"I sure will."

"Oh, Anya," Malaya said before Anya disconnected the call.

"Yeah, what's up, sis?" Malaya looked at the screen at her sister for a few seconds.

"Make Dua (prayer) for me," Malaya said, shutting off her phone. Malaya wiped her eyes, placed the phone back in its hiding place, and removed the cardboard from out of the cell door window. Akeemah saw that Malaya removed the cardboard. She entered into the cell.

"What's wrong, Malaya?" Akeemah asked, seeing tears rolling down Malaya's face. Malaya couldn't answer Akeemah, she was too overwhelmed with tears. Akeemah walked over to Malaya and put her arms around her. They had grown very close over the last few months. The two sisters had built a bond with each other. Sometimes prison does that to people. They draw people near one another because of the circumstances. Akeemah watched Malaya's back and got Malaya back on the path of Islam. Akeemah was back reading her Quran and making the five obligatory prayers.

"Whatever it is that's going on, Malaya, please know that Allah is the overseer of all affairs," Akeemah said, still holding Malaya tight in her arms.

"I like a little girl on girl action. Can I join in?" C.O. Hightower said as he walked into Malaya's cell, catching Malaya and Akeemah in the hugging position.

"Please, not right now," Akeemah pleaded.

"So when is the right time?" Hightower asked, palming his dick through his work slacks.

"It's not right now, Hightower!" Akeemah snapped, grabbed Malaya's hand, and tried to leave the cell. Hightower grabbed Akeemah's arm, stopping her and Malaya.

"When are we going to hook up again?" Hightower asked Akeemah. "I'm tired of fucking Dee-Dee's wack pussy ass." Akeemah looked at Hightower with fire in her eyes.

"We will never hook up again, you slimy dick faggot." Akeemah's statement wounded Hightower's manhood.

"Fuck you, bitch. My dick wasn't slimy when you were drinking my dick juice." Hightower dug his fingertips deeper into Akeemah's arm.

"Just let us go before I scream," Akeemah threatened. Hightower looked at Akeemah with hate.

"You'll be back. They all come back to me. You'll be back in that trash room on your knees sucking me off," Hightower said through clenched teeth. Akeemah yanked away from him.

"Whatever, fuck nigga," Akeemah shot back, exiting the cell with Malaya in tow.

Chapter 22

Velli eased the smoke gray Tahoe through the intersection of Nebraska Avenue and 7th Avenue. The truck belonged to Malaya. He chose to drive it today because he had a sense of need to be close to her, so he drove the truck in hopes that it would satisfy his longing for his wife. Pulling into the parking lot of the Masjid, Velli surveyed the parking lot with a hawk's eye. After the last incident, running into Hakeem, he wasn't taking any risk. Velli knew coming back to this Masjid was dangerous, but Masjid ISTABA was his home. This place of worship did something mentally and spiritually to Velli. Velli could hear the call to prayer being made through the speakers outside the Masjid. Velli slid his kufi (prayer cap) over his studded bald head and, checking his surroundings one last time, he made his way inside the Masjid.

"As Salaam Alaikum, Velli," Iman Basil greeted as he stood inside the entrance of the door.

"Wa Alaikum Salaam," Velli returned the greeting and extended his hand to Iman, who accepted it with a frail hand but firm shake.

"I'm happy to see you today, brother," Iman Basil said with sincerity in his voice.

"Likewise," Velli replied, and headed straight to the restroom. He was avoiding Iman. Velli didn't want to have that sit down with him about what transpired with him and Hakeem and their wives. Velli washed his hands three times and rinsed his mouth and nose out three times. Then he cleaned his arms and feet. He was now ready for prayer. He walked out of the restroom. Velli could see that the brothers were already lined up for prayer, so he joined them and prayed. Velli prayed for his wife. He prayed that Allah would bestow his mercy upon his wife and protect her from the evils of Shayton.

After prayer, Velli just sat there on the floor, trying to enjoy the humble state that ISTABA brought him. Iman Basil came and took a seat next to Velli for a while. He never said a word.

"You know, brother. Allah says in his book that he won't change the conditions of the people until they change the conditions of themselves." Iman Basil then handed Velli a folded piece of paper and left Velli to his thoughts. Velli was in such deep thought about the food of thought that Iman just dropped on him that he almost disregarded the small paper that was handed to him. Velli opened the paper and reviewed its content. The paper held Hakeem's number and the words: Let's talk.

***

"Peaches, what is taking Wayne-Wayne so long to get here?" Splash complained as she grew impatient. "If he's not here in the next ten minutes, I'm leaving. Splash and Peaches stayed low key ever since they had that run in with Mango. They were sure that Mango had some type of hitman out looking for them. Their plan was to leave D.C. and head down to Atlanta and start a new life, but Splash wanted to get rid of the coke she had in the storage. If she could sell every brick for $7,000 a piece times 70, that would give her and Peaches $140,000 plus the $270,000 they got from Stone's safe. The knock at the door alerted the women that Wayne-Wayne was there. Wayne-Wayne had a little crush on Peaches, and he always showed her love when he came through the strip club to see her dance or when she needed some money when she was short on the rent. He always came through for her. She could trust him. Peaches opened the door and was startled to see Wayne-Wayne there with another man. The tall lanky man was eerily looking with all the tattoos covering his body, but before Peaches could protest Wayne-Wayne and his friend were already in the room.

"Hold up, Wayne-Wayne! You were supposed to come by yourself," Splash protested. "Who is this?"

"Chill the fuck out. This is my cousin E-Moe." The name struck a bell and sent off alarms of danger in Splash's head. She just wanted to get the shit over with.

"You got the money?"

"You got the work?" Wayne-Wayne shot back. Splash walked over to the bed, pulled two bricks from under the pillow, and tossed it to Wayne-Wayne. He inspected the product and handed it to E-Moe. E-Moe took one look at the package and saw the red Texas star stamped on the plastic wrapper of the package. E-Moe pulled his Glock 40. "Where the fuck you get the coke from?" E-Moe asked, pointing the gun at Splash. Splash already had heard so much crazy shit about E-Moe and his murderous ways. She stumbled over her words.

"My boyfriend got murdered, and he had it in his coke stash."

"Who the fuck is your boyfriend?" E-Moe questioned.

"Stone." E-Moe couldn't believe how that shit came back full circle. He witnessed Stone get killed by his own brother Mookie. In return, E-Moe and Mario killed Mookie.

"Where the fuck Stone get the coke from?" E-Moe asked, still pointing the gun at Splash.

"He got it from this dude named Mango." Splash was so scared, she didn't know the truth could come from her so freely.

"You know Mango?"

"Yeah, he tried to kill me and Peaches," Splash said, thinking about going for the gun that was in the small of her back. E-Moe smiled at Splash.

"Aye, Wayne-Wayne. Pay the woman," E-Moe said, lowering his gun. Wayne-Wayne gave Splash 14,000 dollars. "Listen, Splash. If Mango tried to kill you then he is an enemy and your enemy is my enemy. I know Mango and the bullshit stunts he tries to pull. I got your back. But, I know it's more coke than this. I'll buy every brick you got, but I want to know everything about this situation from the beginning. Do you understand?" It was time for Splash to smile as she's nodding her head up and down.

Chapter 23

Velli waited patiently in the small coffee house around the corner from the Masjid. He called his brother Damu and explained the situation to him. He had Damu come down to the coffee house to watch his back. Then he placed a call to Hakeem telling him that this was his only chance to talk to him and meet him at the coffee house or the window of talking would be closed forever. Velli did this so Hakeem wouldn't get a chance to plot or ambush him. Hakeem agreed to meet with Velli. Damu sat a few tables away from where Velli was. He wanted to keep his brother in eyesight, but he wanted to be close enough to Velli just in case something jumped off between Hakeem and his brother. Velli and Damu positioned themselves so that they could see the front door of the coffee shop. A very attractive woman came into the coffee shop. Damu thought he knew her from somewhere. He was trying to place her face, but he was too occupied with watching Velli to concentrate on where he had seen the attractive woman before. She stuck out like a hoopty parked on a Bentley car lot. All the women in the coffee shop wore hijabs except her. Hakeem finally entered the coffee shop. Scanning the establishment, his eyes landed on Velli. Velli watched Hakeem make his way over to him.

"Salaam. I come in peace," Hakeem said, not extending his hand to Velli.

"Likewise," Velli said, making a gesture for Hakeem to have a seat. A Muslim sister approached the table to take their order. Both men ordered black coffee. Velli's demeanor rubbed Hakeem the wrong way. "I found these pictures. Do you know any of the dudes that's in them?" Hakeem's phone vibrated in his hand. Hakeem checked his text. It read: To your left is Velli's brother Damu. Hakeem placed the phone on the table.

"Why you want to know about these guys? They both are dead," Velli said with a smirk on his face.

"Yeah, I know that much. I saw the dude Mike's picture on TV. He was found dead in front of my wife's apartment. I'm just trying to find out what Keisha was into while I was in the pen."

"Basically, you are trying to find out why Malaya killed Keisha?"

"Well, yeah, if you want to put it that way."

"Here you go." The waitress came back with Velli and Hakeem's coffee. She sat their cups in front of them and left without even making eye contact with them.

"What you want, the truth, or the sugared down version?" Velli asked.

"I want the truth, Velli," Hakeem said, sliding his coffee cup to the far end of the table. Velli looked out of the window at the car that passed by.

"I don't know what had gotten into Keisha. She was once a loving Muslim sister. Then she changed, and I really don't know what changed your wife because I was behind bars just like you were. I'm just repeating things my wife told me over the years. Keisha was selling drugs with this nigga right here," Velli said, pointing to the picture that held Keisha and Mike in it. Hakeem just listened to Velli with a careful ear. "And this nigga right here is Redz. He was Mike's top man. Keisha and him had a thing for one another when her and Mike went their separate ways because Keisha believed that Malaya wanted Mike. Remember when Muhammad and Anya lost their daughter A'idah in that home invasion while we were doing time in Coleman 2 Penitentiary?"

"Yeah, I remember," Hakeem said, slightly glancing over towards Damu.

"Well, Keisha sent this nigga Redz to rob Malaya thinking that Mike had money stashed at Malaya's house. In the process, Redz raped Anya in front of Anya and Muhammad's eight year old daughter." Velli just shook his head from side to side, thinking about what his wife and Anya had to endure that night. "That's the type of shit that your wife was into," Velli informed Hakeem.

"I don't believe this shit you telling me, Velli. What you telling me is not my wife," Hakeem said in disbelief.

"She even had my nephew kidnapped for ransom money. Keisha is not who you thought she was."

"And if she wasn't, does it make it right for her to die?"

"I didn't say that!" Velli raised his voice a little too loud, making Damu place a hand on the handle of his gun on his waist.

"So what are you saying, Velli?"

"I'm just saying that Keisha was out of control. She was even fucking Muhammad or Steve, whatever you prefer to call him."

"Is that why he was found dead in Keisha's apartment? That's what she died for, huh? Velli, man, this is bullshit!" Hakeem raised his voice, jumping to his feet. "The next time I see you, I hope that you've made your peace with Allah because I'm killing your ass."

Velli looked at Hakeem with a straight face and uttered the words, "Likewise."

Jibril Williams

Loyal to the Soil 3

Chapter 24

45 days later...

"Mrs. Williams, I don't think that you have been truthful with me. There's no report that Keisha had a gun when you shot her," Mr. McCullough said with sternness in his voice.

"I told you that Keisha had a gun, she pointed it at me and tried to kill me, so I had no choice but to shoot her."

"Well, that's not what the report that Officer Bernard Grant turned in said. He is saying that Keisha never had a gun in her possession, and the only gun that was recovered at the crime scene was the one that fired a fatal shot to Ms. Timmons' head." Malaya hung on to every word that Mr. McCullough was saying, trying to detect a lie.

"Mr. McCullough, I'm telling the truth. I swear by Allah that Keisha had a gun," Malaya said, letting out a sigh.

"The psychologist's report came back from the interview she conducted with you. In her report, she deemed that you are fit to stand trial. I was hoping for a self-defense or a stand your ground defense, but without that gun it's going to be hard to do." There was a long silence in the legal room.

"Just let me plea out and get it over with," Malaya mumbled.

"Not so fast, Mrs. Williams. Something may come up. It's still too early to tell, but for right now get that idea out of your mind," Mr. McCullough said, closing his briefcase and standing up from the table, and sliding Malaya a Ziploc bag full of cigarettes. Malaya stuffed the package in her panties and made her way back to her unit. Malaya had so much on her mind, she wondered how the police didn't find Keisha's gun at the crime scene. Some crooked shit was going on in Hillsborough

103

County, but Malaya couldn't understand why, though. Walking into C-block, Malaya saw Dee-Dee and Tiffany coming out of her cell with pillowcases of food. "What the fuck you bitches think you doing? Put my shit back." Malaya ran up on Dee-Dee and Tiffany.

"You know what it is, bitch. It's a robbery," Dee-Dee said, brushing past Malaya.

***

Malaya snatched Dee-Dee by the hair and started kneeing her in the face, like they taught her in the self-defense class that Velli made her attend. The whole C-block could hear Dee-Dee's nose crunch. Dee-Dee fell to the floor. Malaya stomped down on her stomach. Dee-Dee's cellmate named Tiffany ran and attacked Malaya from behind. Ms. Grim couldn't react fast enough. Akeemah was on Tiffany's ass like white on rice. She snatched her by the hair and slapped Tiffany so hard that her nose bled. Tiffany fell down next to Dee-Dee on the floor with no more fight in her. Malaya bent down next to Dee-Dee and whispered, "F.Y.I, bitch. I never been robbed."

Chapter 25

Velli had been stressed the fuck out. His wife was facing murder charges and Hillsborough County was fucking with evidence in Malaya's case, and on top of that, his Muslim brother wanted war with him. Velli drunk the Grey Goose straight from the bottle. He missed Malaya so terribly. He stared at a picture that sat next to his recliner in the living room. The photo displayed Malaya sitting on a sandy beach, where she inscribed Velli's name in the sand. She was being goofy, but the picture came out pretty good. It was one of Velli's favorite pictures of his wife. The ringing of the doorbell brought Velli out of the sadness of missing his wife. Viewing the security monitors on the 80-inch TV screen, he saw that it was Yvette. She had been coming over lately, checking up on him. He staggered to the door and opened it. "Heeey, Yvette," Velli slurred.

"Hey, bay." Yvette threw back at Velli. "Look at you having a party without me."

Yvette pointed to the bottle of Grey Goose in Velli's hand.

"Naw, Yvette. It's not like that, a nigga got problems, you know,"Velli said, swaying on his feet.

"Don't we all?" Yvette agreed with Velli and walked into the house. Yvette seductively walked down the hall towards the living room, lightly dragging her fingertips along the hall wall. Her one-piece tube dress was begging for any man to come fuck her. Velli paid little attention to Yvette. He found his place back into his recliner. Yvette bit down on her lip as she watched Velli in the recliner with his bare feet and chest. His abs flexed as he got comfortable in the chair. She could tell that he was out of it from the drink that he had been consuming. She had never seen Velli drunk. Hell, she had never seen Velli take a drink. "Can I use the bathroom?" Yvette asked.

"Yeah, make yourself at home," Velli replied, taking another sip from his bottle.

"Oh! I plan to," Yvette mumbled under her breath as she made her way upstairs. She loved Velli's house. She couldn't believe that Malaya was dumb enough to kill someone and leave that lovely home behind. "I can see myself living here," Yvette spoke out loud to herself. Walking into the master bedroom, Yvette admired what Malaya had done with the room. She'd been up there a few times before without Velli knowing it. She walked over to the dresser and pulled her tube dress over her head and dropped it to the floor. Yvette looked at herself in the mirror that was over the dresser and admired her body. Her bare nipples rose as she traced her fingertips over them. She picked up Malaya's bottle of coconut Chanel no. 5 and gave herself a spray on the wrist and neck, working it into her skin. *"Now, that's a fragrance that I can get used to,"* Yvette sniffed and thought to herself. She sat her phone on the dresser, set the timer, and went to position herself doggy style on the edge of the bed. She took several different poses, exposing her full breasts. Taking all those pictures in the nude had Yvette dripping wet. Picking up her tube dress, she made her way back downstairs where Velli was still sitting in his recliner with his eyes closed.

***

Malaya massaged Velli's neck as he laid in his beach chair on the beach of Costa Rica. The touch of her small hand felt wonderful on his shoulder and neck. The way that she sucked

106

on his earlobe made his manhood stand at attention. The tropical sun brought sweat upon his body, making it easy for Malaya's soft hands to slide over his bare chest.

"Damn, baby. That feels so good," Velli moaned. Malaya kissed him softly. Tasting the sweet nectar of Malaya's tongue, drove Velli crazy.

"Keep your eyes closed," Malaya whispered. Velli obeyed Malaya's command, wishing and praying that the pleasure would never stop. Malaya gripped his manhood and stroked him slightly through his jeans. She stabbed her tongue in and out of his navel. "Oooh, yes!" Velli coached.

Malaya unzipped his jeans and released his manhood. She kissed the bell pepper shaped head and placed Velli in her mouth, engulfing him whole all the way to the base. She worked her mouth up and down on Velli's massive dick. Velli grabbed the back of her head and worked his hips. Malaya slurped and gagged, coating Velli's manhood with her saliva. Velli couldn't take it anymore. He felt his orgasm. Getting ready to bust, he pumped harder into Malaya's mouth. Malaya fought hard to keep up with Velli's rhythm. His bell pepper shaped head kept slamming into the back of her throat. "I'm coming, baby. I'm cumming," Velli said, opening his eyes. He wasn't in Costa Rica anymore and Malaya wasn't between his legs draining him of his love juices. It was Yvette sucking and draining him away. Velli lost it. "Bitch, get the fuck up!" Velli snatched Yvette by the back of her head. "What the fuck you think you are doing?" Velli said, standing up and putting his manhood back into his jeans. Yvette swallowed Velli's load.

"I thought that's what you wanted," Yvette said, pulling her tube dress over her head and securing it tightly around her flawless body.

"Why in the hell would I want that? I have a wife, and you have a husband."

"And my husband is never coming home, Velli. You know this. Malaya killed someone in front of a police officer. She's never coming home either, Velli. We need each other. We are in the same situation," Yvette said, trying to justify her actions.

"You don't know shit bout my wife or her situation. Now, get the fuck out of our house you silly bitch!" Velli yelled at the top of his lungs. Yvette grabbed her phone off the table that she had propped up against the Grey Goose bottle. Yvette recorded the whole ordeal on her phone. Yvette left in tears and with a broken heart.

Chapter 26

Three days had passed since Malaya had her UFC brawl with Dee-Dee. She hadn't said one word to Jada since then. Malaya was hurt that Jada wasn't there to support her. When Malaya came back into her cell after the fight with her and Jada's belongings with Akeemah in tow, Jada was laying on her bunk reading one of Malaya's books that Anya ordered for her. It was called Bondage by the Hustle by Wollo's Son. Jada laid on her bunk like she didn't have a care in the world. Akeemah wanted to stomp a mudhole in Jada, but Malaya stopped her. Malaya wanted to give herself a few days to heal up before she questioned Jada about her actions. Her body hurt like she'd been run over by a mack truck, but the more Jada remained silent and acted as nothing had happened, it made Malaya madder. Malaya didn't want to make beef with her cellmate because Akeemah was going up for a bond hearing in the next few weeks. The tension was thick between Malaya and Dee-Dee. She and Akeemah stayed strapped at all times with ice picks. A gift that one of the Muslim sisters sold Malaya for a few packs of cigarettes. Malaya sighed. "Let me ask you something, Jada?"

"Go ahead," Jada said, sitting up on her bunk.

"How can you allow someone to come in here and just take your stuff without putting up a fight? I fed you when you didn't have shit. I gave to you when none of these other bitches gave a fuck if you ate or not. How could you not have my back when I was fighting for our shit?" Malaya said, getting angry. Jada put her head down.

"I got my reason."

"Well, give me a reason why I shouldn't snatch your ass off that bunk and whip your ass." Jada jumped down off her bunk.

"I know that I should not let Dee-Dee and Tiffany come in here and violate our cell by taking our things without a fight." Jada folded her arms over her breasts. "But I got other things that are more important to me, Malaya." Jada's eyes started to fill up with tears. Malaya was getting ready to speak, but Jada put her hand up to stop her. "I have twin daughters that really need their mother. My two daughters are living with H.I.V." Tears rolled down Jada's face. "So forgive me if my daughters are more important than some prison commissary. When I was home, I was taking care of my daughters on my own with no help. Their father died in a prison with full blown AIDS. I had no one to watch my children, but I had to work. Therefore, I fed my girls Crystal and Cristian and put them to bed thinking that they would sleep through the night like they had done so many times before." Jada was baring her soul. Malaya stood there crushed, knowing now that Jada had been through so much. "Crystal woke up in the middle of the night hungry." Jada wiped tears from her face. She was only seven. She wanted to make hot dogs like she's seen me do for her and her sister. She pushed a chair to the sink, grabbed a pot from the dish rack, filled it with water, and placed it on the stove. She then went to the fridge, got two hot dogs and placed them in the pot of water. She went back to the stove to get the hot dogs once they were ready. She lost her balance in the chair and knocked the pot of boiling water on her, burning her chest, face, and neck. Jada broke down, weeping uncontrollably. Malaya rushed to her cellmate and hugged her tight.

"Ssssh! It's going to be okay," Malaya spoke in Jada's ear.

"They arrested me and charged me with child neglect. My kids are with my grandmother. I can't afford to get into any trouble. I have a few months left before I get out. My grandmother is really ill. I have to get out, Malaya. I have to get out for my babies," Jada cried out.

"You going to make it, Jada. Four more months and you'll be there," Malaya assured her with teary eyes. Malaya rocked back and forth with Jada in her arms in silence. "Jada, do you have H.I.V. too?"

"Yes," Jada replied, not lifting her head up from Malaya's shoulder.

***

Fatima's mind was heavy, and her heart was cracked in a thousand pieces, like a mirror that's been carelessly knocked down from a wall. She had been trying to clean out her daughter Keisha's room, until she found a bag full of money. She couldn't believe how much money was in the bag. She recognized the bag from when Keisha lugged it into the house the night she was killed. Fatima was puzzled about the money until she found Keisha's diary in the bottom of the bag. Reading the details of her daughter's deepest dark secrets crushed her.

Chapter 27

Bernard Grant sat in the study of his Brandywine home, downing his fourth beer of the night as he watched the 11 o'clock news… "ISIS is gaining a strong hold in Iran," the news reporter reported. "Fuck ISIS! Fuck the Muslims!" Officer Grant yelled at the TV with slurred words, bringing his wife Linda into the study.

"Bernard, what's the matter with you? You're going to wake the kids with all that noise." She scolded him.

"Fuck those Muslim murders. They don't have a strong hold on shit. All the United States has to do is drop a bomb on them like we did Japan and BOOM! All our problems and the Muslims are gone."

"Bernard, you've had too much to drink. Turn the TV off and come to bed," his wife said, shaking her head at him and leaving the room. Bernard had four brothers, and all of them went to fight in the Afghan war. Every last one of them came home with a United States flag draped over their coffin. Just like their father when he went off to fight in the Desert Storm war. Bernard believed that the Muslims wiped out his whole family and that's the reason he hated Muslims, including Malaya Williams. He was going to make her pay for his family's deaths.

***

"What are you going to do, Hakeem?" Iris asked as she watched him clean and load the guns she helped him get from one of her homeboys. Hakeem took about 80 thousand from the bag of money that he found in Keisha's room and stashed the rest back under her bed.

"I'm going to kill Velli's bitch ass."

"And, just throw your life away again?" Iris shot back at Hakeem, her words cutting him deep.

"His wife killed my wife, so I'm killing his ass."

"What's that going to prove? Either you're going to die trying to kill Velli, or you're going to jail forever." Iris had seen this story play out too many times before.

"Bitch, you acting like you taking up for Velli and Malaya."

"No, I'm not! But, my cousin is gone and nothing that you do is going to bring her back. The person who killed her is in jail, and she's going to be there forever." Iris got out of bed and sat in front of Hakeem. "Listen, baby. I know that you are hurting and over time your wounds will heal." Iris looked at Hakeem with pleading eyes.

"This is the only way that I know how to heal," Hakeem said cocking his Mack 11.

"Do you think Velli doesn't know you're going to come at him? That's why his brother Damu was there at the coffee shop."

"Yeah. He knows I'm coming, but he don't know how I'm coming," Hakeem said with a smirk on his face.

"You are just one man, Hakeem. Velli is going to have people protecting his back and ready to die for him at his beck and call."

"Don't sweat. Allah have my back."

"If you really believe that, then let Allah handle it for you," Iris said, becoming frustrated with Hakeem. She got up and walked to the door. Hakeem, don't do this." Hakeem never responded. He just kept cleaning his gun.

Chapter 28

Malaya had just gotten through offering her noon prayer on the back of the tier with Akeemah. The two sisters had grown inseparable since the fight with Dee-Dee and her cellmate. They watched each other's backs. When Malaya was in the shower, Akeemah stood guard and vice versa. Even when one of them had to use the bathroom, the other one was right outside the door. Akeemah slightly elbowed Malaya in the side, getting her attention that they had a set of eyes on them. Malaya turned around and saw a plump sister leaning on the rail of the tier watching them. Malaya and Akeemah had a lot of admirers since they beat Dee-Dee and Tiffany's asses.

"Hi." The plump woman greeted Malaya and Akeemah. Akeemah never acknowledged the woman verbally, she just sized the woman up.

"Hi, what's up?" Malaya asked.

"Oh, nothing. I was just watching you pray."

"Why?" Akeemah broke her silence for the first time. Malaya elbowed her.

"It just seemed so peaceful and humbling." The woman smiled. "Why do you pray so much?"

"Well, let me say this first," Malaya replied. If you had a river in front of your house, and you took a bath in it five times a day, would there be any traces of dirt on your body?" The woman thought about what Malaya was saying.

"No, there would not be any traces of dirt if I bathed five times a day."

Well, praying five times a day is equal to bathing five times a day. Bathing washes the dirt from you. Prayer washes away the sins." Malaya smiled.

"Oh, I get it," the woman said, smiling.

"Malaya Williams!" C.O. Hightower yelled.

"Yeah!" Malaya yelled from the back of the tier.

"You have a legal visit. Get ready. You have five minutes."

"Okay!" Malaya turned her attention back to the plump woman. "What's your name?"

"Oh, I'm Angie."

"Well, I'm Malaya. Anytime you want to talk about Islam, I'm here, but right now, I got to get ready for this legal visit. So get with me later."

Malaya went to her cell. She brushed her teeth and grabbed her legal folder. She was escorted to the visiting room by Officer Hightower. "So when are you going to let me get some of that pussy, Malaya?"

"Never! I don't be tricking, and I don't fuck with police and low lifers that take advantage of women because they got the upper hand on them."

"All you bougie bitches are just the same. You all come to jail and think your pussy still holds the same value as it did when you were in the streets. I'll break you before it's all said and done," Hightower said as he stepped in front of the visiting room door and asked control to crack it. The door slid to the side and Malaya stepped through it, following behind Hightower. They had to travel down a short hall to actually reach the legal visiting room.

Malaya checked in at the desk at the end of the hall. "Name?" the guard asked.

"Malaya Williams."

"Your attorney is waiting in room 5 around the corner." Hightower could have gone back to C-block, but he couldn't get enough of watching Malaya's ass sway side to side, so his perverted ass followed Malaya all the way to visiting room 5. Malaya walked into the small visiting room and froze. She couldn't believe who was sitting at the small table with Mr. McCullough.

"Velli!?" C.O. Hightower yelled. "Is that you?"

"Muthafucka! Coby Hightower." Velli jumped up and embraced Hightower. "Man it's been years since the last time that I've seen you. How is your moms?"

"She's good. She's still alive and kicking," Hightower said, as he let Velli go from their embrace. "Damn, you are a lawyer now?"

"Naw, I'm a private investigator. He's the lawyer," Velli said, pointing at Mr. McCullough. Malaya just took a seat and watched in awe. "Look, man. Give me your number, and we can hook up some time this week." Hightower jotted his number down on a piece of paper and made Velli promise that he would give him a call and left. Velli closed the door behind Hightower.

Soon as the door closed and Hightower walked away, Malaya jumped in Velli's arms, wrapping her legs around his waist. She stuck her tongue so deep in Velli's mouth that she could feel his tonsils. Velli kissed his wife back with so much passion. He almost forgot that Mr. McCullough was in the room. Malaya pulled away from Velli's lips. "How you pull this off, baby?"

"That Blackstone paralegal course that I took when I was in the Feds. I'm certified to be a paralegal an investigator. So, Mr. McCullough hired me to work at his firm," Velli said with a smile. Mentioning her lawyer's name, Malaya realized he was still in the room.

"Oh. Hi, Mr. McCullough."

"Hi, Mrs. Williams. Look, you two only have fifteen minutes. I know the female C.O. that's at the desk down the hall. I'm going to go keep her occupied until you two do your thing. 15 minutes!" Mr. McCullough said with a stern face and walked out of the door. Velli wasted no time unbuttoning his pants that released his long throbbing manhood. Malaya attempted to get on her knees to devour Velli's long Mandingo.

"No, baby. We don't have time for that," Velli said, stopping her. Malaya undid her orange jumper, letting it hit the floor along with her panties. She positioned herself, bent over the table that was in the legal visiting room, and arched her back.

"Come get it, baby," she whispered.

Velli pulled the foreskin back and squeezed the base of his manhood, making his bell pepper head swell to the size of a golf ball. Inserting himself into Malaya, she was a tight fit. She gasped loudly as Velli pushed the base inside of her. "Oh, baby. I miss you so much. I miss this pussy so damn much. Do you miss this dick, baby?" Velli asked, picking up his pace as he began to pound Malaya from the back.

"Ooooo, yes! Baby, I miss this dick. Give it to me, baby. Please give it to me," Malaya coached her husband. She could feel her orgasm building up, and she began to throw her ass back into Velli. She met his every thrust.

Velli gripped Malaya's ass cheeks firmly and spread them apart as he thrust into her, watching Malaya's juices coat his shaft. "Here it comes, baby!" Velli announced that he was cumming. Velli let out a loud grunt as he pushed down deep inside of Malaya and shot a heavy load in her. Malaya's thighs shook as she released her own love juices. She rocked back and forth on Velli's centerpiece until he emptied everything that he had in her.

Chapter 29

Malaya laid in her bed thinking about her sexual encounter with her husband. The thoughts were so overwhelming that she had to get up twice from her daydream and wipe the dripping moistness from between her legs. Malaya bit down on her bottom lip, mentally re-living how Velli's love muscle invaded her walls. She had a brief talk with Velli about his boy Coby Hightower and how he had been trying to push up on her and take advantage of the women on C-block. Velli was 38 Special hot. He promised that she would never have to worry about Hightower messing with her again. Mr. McCullough informed her that she would have a status hearing in the next forty days. He would ask for a bond. Mr. McCullough and Velli tossed around the theory on how Keisha's gun came up missing, but none of their theories made any sense. The only thing that made sense about the matter was that Bernard Grant was holding back evidence. But "why" was the question, and how could they prove it was the million-dollar question.

"As Salaam Alaikum, Malaya!" Akeemah said as she and Jada walked into the cell. Akeemah had embraced Jada after Malaya revealed Jada's situation to her. All three women had built a special kind of bond with each other.

"Salaam, sister!" Malaya said, still laying on her bunk.

"Girl, you laying there all tango'd up in them sheets like you just got dicked down or something. Girl, look at cha. You all glowing and shit," Akeemah said.

"Girl, only if you knew!" Malaya replied and jumped from under the sheet and sat on the edge of her bunk.

"Girl, what are you talking about?" Jada butted in.

"Nothing," Malaya said, switching the subject. "What we eating tonight?"

"I don't know. I can't eat nothing right now. I have my bond hearing in the morning, and I'm so nervous," Akeemah said, wiping her sweaty hands on her jumper.

"Oh, that's right. I forgot about that," Malaya replied. Thinking to herself that Dee-Dee and her crew were going to want some payback if Akeemah made it out on the bond hearing. The tension on C-block was still thick between them.

"Yeah, I know the people at court not going to give me a bond. If they do, it's going to be a bond that I can't afford." Akeemah rolled her eyes at the thought.

"Akeemah, you got to trust in Allah. He will help you overcome the unthinkable," Malaya said, getting up from her bunk and sliding her feet in her Reebok classics. "Now let's go find Angie, so we can play some spades," Malaya said, leading the women out of the cell into the day room to look for Angie.

***

E-Moe had been moving work like crazy. The extra shipment Velli sent from Mango had him making moves non-stop. He expanded his business to Alexander, VA, right on the outskirts of D.C. to handle the large shipments that came in. Making this move was fruitful. The money was coming in by the truck load. E-Moe had been so busy in the last few weeks that he had not had a chance to reveal his findings to Velli about Splash and Mango. As he laid in bed, he thought since he was not up and mobile at the time, that he should give Velli a call. E-Moe grabbed his phone off the nightstand and hit Velli on speed dial. The phone rang once before Velli picked up.

"What's up, Slim?" Velli said. Velli had not been back in D.C. since the night Stone and his brother Mookie died.

"You know if it don't make dollars, it don't make sense."

"Yeah, I hear ya, but what's the reason for the early morning call?"

"I have something you may want to hear."

"Alright drop it on me then, Slim."

E-Moe told Velli everything that Splash told him about Mango coming to D.C. hoping to find his shipment of drugs that he shipped to Stone days before he was murdered. He even told Velli of his plan to get rid of Mango. Velli was all ears and loved every bit of what was being said.

"Damn, E-Moe. I figure that fat muthafucka been to D.C. because he asked me about Stone and Mookie's murders."

"Do you think he knows you had something to do with the hit on Stone?"

"He pretty much knows that I had something to do with it, but he can't prove it," Velli said, flipping the TV to ESPN. "So, what's up with the bitch Splash?"

"I got her on lockdown. She's in Atlanta. When it's time to put our plan together, I'll call her back to D.C."

"So she's game tight like that, huh?" Velli asked.

"Hell, yeah. I'm fucking and feeding her all the love lines about being the queen bitch in my life, but if push comes to shove, we can bag and tag her." E-Moe laughed into the phone.

"Alright. You know that you are a wild ass nigga for that, right? I like the sound of it. Just keep her close until we pull this off."

"Okay, Slim. Bet that up," E-Moe said through the phone.

"And remember, E-Moe. Loyalty over everything," Velli said and disconnected the call.

Chapter 30

Fatima was in turmoil as she sipped her tea. She really couldn't believe the things she read in her daughter Keisha's diary. Keisha was living a very wicked life. She had multiple sex partners, four abortions, murderous plots, and anything you could name and think of; Keisha had jotted it down in her diary. Some were in lengthy details and some weren't. Fatima didn't know what to think of her daughter at the moment. As she sipped her tea, Fatima thought back to the days when Keisha was a young girl. Fatima's eyes started to fill up with tears. That's all she'd been doing since she found the diary was shed tears. *"How could my little girl turn so rotten and poisonous?"* Fatima thought to herself.

"Salaam, Fatima," Hakeem said as he entered the kitchen.

"Salaam, Hakeem," Fatima replied, wiping her tears from her face.

"Why are you crying?" Hakeem asked with great concern.

"I found a bag full of money in Keisha's room the other day." Hakeem knew exactly what bag of money she was talking about. "And in the bag I found Keisha's diary, and it had some real sickening stuff in it," Fatima said, still wiping tears from her eyes.

"Can I read it?" Hakeem asked, walking over to Fatima and placing his hands on her shoulders.

"No! It's full of filth."

"Please, Fatima. Let me have it. It may answer some of the questions that I have."

"She did it, Hakeem. She really did it."

"Did what, Fatima?" Hakeem asked, looking confused.

"She had that child kidnapped. She kidnapped Anya's son." The money that was in the bag with the diary was ransom money. It was the money that she got from the kidnapping."

"No, Fatima. This can't be true. What you are telling me is not the Keisha that I knew."

"It's her, Hakeem. It's all in the diary."

"I'm not going to believe that!" Hakeem raised his voice.

"You can believe what you want, but I saw my daughter bring that same bag into my house the night before she was murdered. It's her handwriting in the diary, Hakeem. I feel so bad for Malaya."

"For Malaya? She killed my wife. She killed your daughter," Hakeem said, wide-eyed and through clenched teeth. "How dare you feel sorry for her?"

"I don't feel sorry for her, but Malaya was just protecting her family from Keisha. I got to go talk to the police. When they came to my house the night my daughter was murdered, I told them that Malaya and Anya came to my house looking for Keisha armed with guns. I never told the police about Malaya and Anya mentioning that Keisha had kidnapped Anya's son.

"You are not going to the cops about shit!" Hakeem squeezed down on the back of Fatima's neck. "Now, give me the diary," he demanded. Fatima felt a flash of pain shoot up the back of her neck from Hakeem's grip. She yelled out in pain.

"Awwwwe! Hakeem, the diary is over there in the top kitchen drawer." Hakeem released Fatima and retrieved the diary.

"I'm going to make Velli pay for allowing Malaya to kill my wife."

***

"That's a seven-letter word that I just dropped and that's game," Jada boasted.

"Damn, you are scrabble playing muthafucka," Angie said with a smile. Malaya bust out laughing.

"Look, I got to go use the bathroom, Jada. Come watch the door," Malaya said.

"I'm coming, too," Angie said, getting up from the table in the dayroom and followed Malaya and Jada to their cell. Angie was aware of the tension between Dee-Dee and Malaya. She didn't care too much for Dee-Dee because she was a bully and preyed on the weak. Before Anya went to court that morning, she had a talk with Jada. She told Jada to watch Malaya's back and whatever happened to Malaya while she was gone better happen to her too because she would have wished it did if she came back from court and something had happened to Malaya. Jada promised her that she would hold Malaya down if it came down to it. Malaya didn't really have to use the bathroom. She really wanted to go call Velli real quick to let him know that she was missing him and to see if she could make an appointment next week for some good loving. Malaya went into her cell, placed the flap up in the window of her cell door, and got the IPhone out of her stash spot. She dialed her husband. The phone rang four times before it went to voicemail. Malaya tried two more times, and she got the same results. She sent Velli a text saying that she missed and loved him so much. Malaya noticed that she had six missed texts and a video pending. She didn't recognize the number, but she opened the text anyway. Malaya's heart fell to the pit of her stomach. Malaya started looking at the small frame and round ass in the doggy style position. Malaya couldn't believe that Velli would have that woman in their home in their bed. There was a message attached to the photo. It read: You snooze, you lose. Malaya checked the other waiting texts, and they were all the same. Some woman was posed in a sexual position in her bedroom. Malaya didn't recognize the woman because she couldn't see the bitch's face. By now, Malaya was in full tears. *"How could Velli betray me like this?"* she thought to herself. Malaya looked at another one of the videos. She had to bite down on her hand to keep from screaming out. The video displayed Velli sitting in his favorite recliner, getting his manhood deep throated by a naked woman.

Chapter 31

Velli pulled the Range Rover in the back of Roberts Projects. Coby Hightower sat in the passenger seat, with Velli's brother Damu sitting right behind him. They took Coby out to explore the city, and they hit a few crap tables at the casino in St. Pete. They also went to a few strip clubs and lo and behold, Coby acted a damn fool. He was a vicious booty hound. Velli and Damu let him trick with every stripper he desired to be with. One girl at the club that Damu knew revealed that Coby liked for the strippers to stick their finger in his butt, and he also liked licking ass.

"So what are we doing next, Velli?" Coby asked all hyped up. And what are you doing in the hood?" Before Velli could answer, Damu dropped a thick plastic bag over Coby's head from the backseat and pulled tight. Velli just sat there bobbing his head to the new Young Jeezy album titled, Church in These Streets. Coby clawed at the bag, trying to get some air into his lungs. He felt lightheaded. He violently fought hard to get free.

"Damu, let this nigga go," Velli ordered, turning the music down in the truck. Velli's phone vibrated in his lap. Coby gasped to get air in his lungs. Slob dripped from his mouth.

"Man, what the fuck!" Coby yelled, grabbing his throat and trying to gain his composure. Velli pulled his 40 caliber out and pointed it in Coby's face.

"Open your mouth, nigga," Velli said with a look of hatred on his face. Velli's phone vibrated in his lap again. Coby, still trying to catch his breath, obeyed Velli's orders and opened his mouth. "Now listen, real careful. Malaya Williams that lives on C-block is my wife. She told me that you have been pushing up on her, trying to fuck her." Velli pushed the gun deeper into Coby's mouth with a little force.

"From now on Malaya, Akeemah, Jada, and whoever else my wife says is off limits. Do you hear me?" Coby nodded his head up and down with Velli's gun still in his mouth.

"And as of today, you work for me. I'll tell you what to bring my wife, and I'll pay you."

"No is not an option for you. Do you get it?" Coby still just moved his head up and down, looking scared out of his mind. "I can't believe you, Coby. Taking advantage of them women. If I didn't go to school with you and know your mother, I would have killed your punk ass," Velli said, putting the truck in drive to take Coby back home.

***

Malaya laid facing the wall, crying her eyes out when Akeemah walked in her cell. "Malaya, what's wrong with you?" Akeemah was concerned for her friend.

"I don't want to talk about it now. Akeemah, please don't pry," Malaya said, still facing the wall as she talked to Akeemah. "What happened in court today? Did you get the bond?"

"Yeah, I got the bond," Akeemah said with great sadness.
"How much is it?"

"The judge knows that it was not my gun in that rental car, but being that I wouldn't cooperate with the government and tell that it was Yah-Yah's gun, the judge punished me by giving me a $30,000 bond. He gave me that bond because he knew that I couldn't pay it. I'm so frustrated. I could use some green tea." That was it for Malaya, she now knew who the woman in the pictures could've possibly been that was sent on her phone.

"You want to bond out, Akeemah?" Malaya asked.
"Hell, yeah! But I don't have the money."

"Don't worry about it. I got the money. I just need you to take care of some shit for me when you get out. I need someone's ass whipped, "Malaya said, getting her phone out, and calling her #1 road dawg.

"Hello," Anya answered on the second ring.

"It's me, Malaya. I need a favor from you."

Anya heard the seriousness in her sister's voice and said,

"Anything for you, sister."

"My Muslim sister has a $30,000 bond. I need it paid. Remember how we handled Keisha after Ai'dah's death?" Anya fell silent for a few seconds.

"Yeah, I remember."

"Well, same shit but just a different bitch," Malaya said, going on to explain the situation to Malaya while Akeemah listened.

Jibril Williams

Chapter 32

Velli blew up Malaya's phone after he finally received the photos of Yvette naked in their bed. He couldn't come up with an excuse as to why and how Yvette could take the pictures, but what was really tearing at him was that he couldn't explain to Malaya why Yvette had his manhood in her mouth on video. It happened, but it wasn't what he wanted or his intention. He didn't want Malaya sitting in jail thinking that he betrayed her. He couldn't imagine what was going through Malaya's mind right then. He took another gulp from the Grey Goose bottle. The clear liquor burned his throat as it went down. He dialed Malaya's number again. Velli had been calling her every fifteen minutes, trying to get a hold of her. The phone rang six times before it went to voicemail. "Come on, baby. Answer the phone," Velli talked out loud to himself as he tried to call Malaya again. He remembered that almost four years ago he sat inside Coleman Penitentiary and received some photos of Malaya and Mike together laying naked on a floor at Keisha's house. And the thoughts that went through his mind were chilling. He knew that Malaya was going through it. Come to find out, those pictures were staged by Keisha. Come to find out Keisha had drugged Malaya and let Mike have his way with Malaya. Malaya eventually understood this was a similar situation. Velli took another gulp of the Grey Goose. Malaya refused to give up on them when Velli received the pictures of her and Mike, even though Velli didn't want to have anything else to do with her after that. So, Velli must take the same stance Malaya took and not give up on Malaya because she did not fully understand the circumstances of the situation. He dialed Malaya's number again. "Come on, baby. Answer the phone."

***

Akeemah walked out of Hillsborough County Jail as a free woman. It took the sheriff forever to process her paperwork. The midnight air was cool on her skin. She was thankful that she was free. She walked a few blocks until she could catch a cab. She had $80 in her belongings when she was arrested. Upon discharging from the jail, the money was still in her Chanel purse. Akeemah wore 90 day old clothes, the same clothes she wore the night she was arrested. Right then, all she wanted to do was get home and take a long hot bath in her own bathtub. Then tomorrow she was going to call Anya to see about handling that business for Malaya. Finally, a cab stopped for Akeemah. She gave the cab driver her address and a $20 bill and rested her head on the backseat of the headrest. Her thoughts turned to how Yah-Yah badly treated her. She was broken-hearted and angry at the same time. *"How could he just abandon me like I don't mean shit to him?"* Akeemah thought to herself. She knew that was the last straw for Yah-Yah. She would have to cut him loose. The cab pulled in the front of a small brick house on Nedro Drive. Akeemah exited the cab and made her way into her house. The weed scent invaded her nose. She could hear music coming from the back of the house. She knew that Yah-Yah was home. Walking in the living room, she stopped in her tracks when she saw the large stacks of money on the table. *"Yah-Yah must've found him a victim to rob. That's the only time he has that kind of money,"* Akeemah thought to herself. "Oh! Yes, baby. Oh, yes!" Akeemah heard a female's voice from the back of the house. "I know that this fuck nigga don't have a bitch in my house," Akeemah mumbled and snatched one of the guns that was on the table next to money, and headed towards the back of the house. Thrusting the bathroom door open, where the music was coming from, Yah-Yah sat in the tub with some white girl riding his dick. Yah-Yah's eyes got bigger than a full moon on a dark night when he saw Akeemah standing in the doorway clutching his burner.

"Hold up, baby. I can explain," Yah-Yah stuttered.

"You can't explain shit to me. I can see what's going on from where I'm standing," Akeemah said, pointing the gun at Yah-Yah and the white girl.

"Hold up, baby," Yah-Yah protested while trying to ease the white girl off his dick.

"Don't move, bitch," Akeemah threatened. "You left me in jail to rot for you. You didn't send me no assistance. No lawyer, no food, no letters, no phone calls, and now you bring a bitch in my house. You going to sit in my face and beg me to spare you and this funky ass bitch?" Akeemah walked closer to the tub. Trey Songz sang from the CD player that sat on the edge of the tub.

"Baby, just listen to me. We just pulled a lick. I know you seen all that money on the table in there. I was going to come get you out of jail in the morning. Baby, I swear." Akeemah wanted to believe Yah-Yah so bad, but the evidence was right in her face.

"Tell that shit to the devil in hell you rotten muthafucka," Akeemah said as she kicked the CD player into the tub, sending Yah-Yah and his white girl to a terrible death. Akeemah went into the living room and threw the money in a bag, along with two guns. She wiped everything down that she touched and left. She left unheard and unseen.

Jibril Williams

134

Chapter 33

Malaya dialed Yvette's number that she had attached to the photos that she sent her.

"She attached her number for a reason, so she must want me to call her," Malaya said to herself. She put the phone next to her ear.

"Hello, Malaya. I see that you got my lovely pictures in my beautiful home," Yvette teased followed by a loud laugh.

"Bitch, fuck you! That's my house. It will never be yours," Malaya shot back at Yvette.

"Your house became mine when you decided to leave that luscious home and go kill that poor little girl. You have to be one of the dumbest bitches I know to do some crazy shit like that." The words hit Malaya hard, but she wasn't going to reveal that to Yvette.

"Sorry, baby. I'm never a dumb bitch, and you're a dumb bitch to even think I'm going to let you get away with disrespecting me like this. I'm like the fucking MOB! My arms reach beyond these walls." Malaya raised her voice a little louder. Jada had to peep her head in the cell and let Malaya know that she could be heard on the tier.

"Pssss! Please girl, I'm not worried about you. You need to worry about doing that life sentence they are going to give your funky ass." Yvette's words cut Malaya deep again. Malaya fell silent. "While you will be doing life, I'll be sucking the life out of Velli, bitch." Yvette said, laughing into the phone.

"You know what, Yvette? You got that, but I will have the last laugh, and you can trust me on that. I will have the last laugh," Malaya said with tears in her voice as she disconnected the call with Yvette. Malaya was crushed, Yvette said some true shit on the phone. She knew that she was facing some major time for killing Keisha, and she needed to focus on that and not worry about who Velli was fucking. The only way that she could do her time without distractions was to cut ties with Velli. She hit Velli's number on speed dial. Velli answered on the second ring.

"Hello, Malaya!" Velli's voice boomed through the phone.

"Yeah."

"Baby, please listen to me. Things are not as what they seem. I had nothing to do with that bitch, I was half drunk out of my mind. I had no intentions of doing anything with her." Velli rambled on, trying to find the right combination of words to reach Malaya's heart.

"You hurt me, Velli," Malaya whispered as the tears rolled down her cheeks.

"I know, baby, but I was -"

"Just listen, Velli," Malaya cutting him off in mid-sentence. "I have time to do, Velli. You know that it's going to be a long time before we ever walk the streets together again."

"No, Malaya. Just hold up."

"No, you hold up. I can't be in here and be worrying about you and the next bitch you are with. You're going to be a man and when the queen is away the king will play." Malaya wiped tears from her face. "I want a divorce. I don't ever want to see you or hear from you again."

"I can't do that, Malaya. I just can't do that," Velli pleaded.

"If you truly love me, you can, and you will. I forgive you for what you did. Just honor my wishes." Malaya disconnected the call with Velli and stashed the phone back into the mattress. Malaya needed a long hot shower. She grabbed her shower bag, towel, and shower shoes and made her way to the shower.

"Are you okay?" Jada asked.

"Yeah, I'm good. Let me take a shower, then when I come back, you can use the phone to call the twins."

"Ok, that will be great." Jada smiled just thinking about hearing her daughters' voices.

"Hightower is bringing us in subway sandwiches tonight."

"Damn, that nigga been bringing us food every night this week," Jada said, following Malaya to the shower area to keep post while Malaya took a shower.

"Yeah, those are the benefits when you know somebody that knows something about it," Malaya said with a slight smile. Malaya felt someone watching her. She looked up on the top tier and two sets of eyes were on her. They belonged to Dee-Dee and a woman that looked familiar to her. Dee-Dee and the Amber Rose looking sister were staring at her with their faces balled up like they smelled shit. "Jada, who is the bitch that Dee-Dee is talking to?"

"I don't know. She came in while you was on the IPhone. The word is she came from A-block. She probably was transferred to C-block to get up under C.O. Hightower. You know how bitches are," Jada said, peeping up at Dee-Dee and her new friend.

"Watch that bitch around me. She's sending off bad vibes," Malaya said, walking back to the shower.

"I got you, boss lady," Jada said, but hoping that it wouldn't come down to that.

Jibril Williams

Chapter 34

Standing in front of Judge Karen Jackson on weak legs, Malaya heard her lawyer argue back and forth about giving his client a bond. The prosecutor, Samantha Davis, insisted that Malaya was a flight risk and if given a bond, she would flee and prolong the trial.

"The motion for bond is denied," Judge Jackson said with emphasis, letting Mr. McCullough know that Malaya wasn't getting a bond under no circumstances, so move on to setting a trial date.

"Your Honor," Mr. McCullough said, adjusting his tie. "What is the government offering my client if she is willing to take a plea?"

"Is Mrs. Williams pleading guilty?"

"It all depends on what the government is offering." Prosecutor Samantha Davis shuffled through some papers.

"Your Honor, the government is offering a plea of 25 years if Mrs. Williams cooperates with us and reveals who committed the other murders at Keisha Timmons' home."

Mr. McCullough leaned over and whispered in Malaya's ear.

"What do you want to do, Mrs. Williams?"

"Fuck them. I'm not a snitch, tell them bitches let's go to trial. Tell them to let me go," Malaya said a little too loud, letting the prosecutor hear her and turning her beet red.

"Well, let's give them hell, Mrs. Williams." He faced the judge. "Your Honor, we would like to set a trial date," Mr. McCullough said, writing some notes down on his legal pad.

"You have 90 days, Mr. McCullough, since Mrs. Williams thinks we are bitches, and she is no snitch."

"Your Honor, I can't prepare for a case such as this on such short notice," Mr. McCullough complained.

"You have 90 days, Mr. McCullough. Do you agree, Ms. Davis?"

"Yes, that's fine with me. The sooner, the better."

"Well then, November 15th is the trial start date," Judge Jackson said, banging her gavel and moving on to the next case. Velli, Damu, Anya, and Akeemah sat in the back of the courtroom. Velli prayed that Malaya would look his way and make eye contact with him, but Malaya never turned her head his way. Malaya was serious about not speaking to him again, and she wasn't the only one, either. Anya had not said a word to him since she found out about the Yvette incident. He would catch Anya looking at him with murder in her eyes, then she would just shake her head and look the other way. Velli tried to explain to her, but Anya wasn't hearing it. If her husband wasn't his brother, Anya would probably try to kill him. Velli got up and walked out of the courtroom, catching up with Malaya's lawyer. "Mr. McCullough! Hold up."

"What's up, Velli?" Mr. McCullough said.

"Man, they are not cutting Malaya no slack I see," Velli said depressed.

"It seems that way."

"How can I help, Mr. McCullough?" Mr. McCullough looked around the court building, then pulled Velli close so no one else could hear what was being said.

"She only has one eyewitness to the crime, and you already know who that is." Mr. McCullough gave Velli a stern look and walked away.

Chapter 35

Three weeks later… Yvette pulled up in front of her three-bedroom duplex. She was a little buzzed from tonight's event at Felicitous Coffee & Tea House. One of her regulars threw a birthday party there, and the pink champagne was plentiful. Yvette got out of her car and looked at her duplex. Loneliness came over her. Her man, Chief, had been locked up for eight years now, and she was tired of coming home to an empty house and a cold bed. The thought of being alone another night brought her watery eyes. She stumbled towards her duplex. Velli's handsome face appeared in her mind. It was something about the man that made Yvette act out of character, but she just had to have him. She felt bad about how things went down between her and Malaya, but Malaya was stupid enough to go out in the streets and kill someone when she should have been home sexing Velli down. Yvette giggled out loud on her thought of Velli's manhood. *"Shit, I'm going to call him and see if he is still mad at me, and if he's not then, I'm inviting him over for some of this wet pussy,"* Yvette thought to herself as she stuck her key into the cylinder of her door and unlocked her front door. The hard blow to Yvette's head made her stubble into her house. "Aggg." Yvette let out a cry of pain from the blow. She heard the door behind her close. She rolled over on her back to stare up at two female figures in black hoods.

"Bitch, didn't I tell your dirty ass if I caught you around my sister's house again, I was going to whip that ass?" Anya said, staring down at Yvette. Yvette looked up from the floor wide-eyed. Akeemah stomped hard into Yvette's stomach, knocking the air out of her.

"You heard her. Answer the fucking question!" Akeemah barked. Yvette struggled to gain her breath and formulate words in her mouth.

"I'm - I'm sorry," Yvette whispered.

"Oh, your ass going to be sorry. Your trashy ass boasted to my friend about fucking her husband. You found that cute, huh?" Akeemah said, grabbing Yvette by the hair while Anya cut her clothes off her body.

"Please stop! I'm sorry ... Please stop," Yvette begged. Anya slapped Yvette so viciously that she saw stars. Yvette laid there on the floor in a fetus position, crying. Akeemah grabbed her phone out of her pocket and dialed a number. Moments later, Malaya's face appeared on the screen. Akeemah FaceTime'd her.

"Malaya, we got the bitch," Akeemah said into the screen of the IPhone.

"Well, let me talk to her."

"Yvette, someone wants to talk to you," Akeemah said from over top of her. Yvette peeped out from her fetus position and saw Malaya staring at her through the screen of Akeemah's phone.

"Awwww! Look at you now. Butt naked and scared just like a baby," Malaya taunted Yvette. "I told you I was like the fucking MOB and my arms reached beyond these prison walls, but you didn't believe me. What do have to say now, bitch?"

"I'm sorry!" Yvette blabbed out in tears. "You can have Velli," Yvette rambled on. "He never wanted me. Please, just look at the entire video on my phone. Please. I will never approach Velli again." Anya went into Yvette's purse, retrieved her phone, and placed it in her pocket.

"Naw, fuck that. You can have Velli. You can wait in hell for him. Akeemah, kill that bitch!" Malaya ordered.

Akeemah struck Yvette with the same lead pipe she hit her with when coming into the house. The pipe savagely came

Loyal to the Soil 3

down on Yvette's head, cracking her skull. Akeemah continued to viciously beat Yvette until her body laid there lifeless while Anya looked in awe. Anya knew she was crazy, but Akeemah was a whole different type of crazy, but she liked her style. The whole time Akeemah beat Yvette, she thought about how Yah-Yah dogged her out for a white girl.

"Akeemah!" Anya had to call her to bring her back to reality. Akeemah was covered in blood and her chest was rapidly going up and down. "We got to get out of here," Anya said, walking to the door. Akeemah followed behind her, picking up Yvette's keys off the floor. Back in the car, Akeemah changed clothes, cleaned herself up with baby wipes, and then placed it in a plastic bag. Anya pulled in the alley behind Felicitous Coffee and Tea House. This was the establishment that Yvette and Velli owned together. Anya and Akeemah made their way through the back door with the keys Akeemah picked up off of Yvette's floor. The back door let them into the kitchen. The crime partners moved fast. Anya blew out all the lights, opened the stove and oven, and let the gas escape freely throughout the kitchen. Akeemah lit five candles and threw the plastic bag with the bloody clothes in it on the stove. They made their way back out the back door and drove away. Two blocks away, they both heard a loud explosion and felt the ground shake under them. They both knew their plan had worked. "Oh, here," Akeemah said, handing Anya a brown paper bag full of money.

"What's this for?" Anya looked confused.

"That's for the money you loaned me to bond out of jail with."

Anya smiled. "Naw, Akeemah. We are family now. That's yours, keep it." Anya handed Akeemah back the money.

Chapter 36

Splash sat nervously outside Mason Storage Space out in P.G. County in Maryland outside of D.C. She finally broke down, called Mango, and told him that she wanted no problem with him or his people. She also told him that she was willing to give him back the drugs that he had shipped to Stone and Mookie if he promised not to hurt her. Mango agreed that he wouldn't hurt her if she gave the 100 keys back. Splash convinced him that she didn't trust nobody else to come to get the drugs but him. Mango was hesitant, but the cartel back in Mexico were finally starting to breathe down his neck about the decrease in his purchase from them, and they wanted to know why. So, Mango had no other choice but to go to Maryland and pick the drugs up himself. Splash's palms got sweaty as she saw Mango pull up behind her in his truck with his driver, Pappay. Mango got out of the truck and made his way to Splash's car. She rolled the window down. "Follow me," Splash said.

"Hold up!" Mango reached in the car, felt around Splash's neck, and raised the front of her shirt up.

"You think that I'm wearing a wire or something?" Splash rolled her eyes at Mango.

"I'd rather be safe than sorry. If you got some bullshit up your sleeve, I'm killing your whore ass today, Mommi," Mango said, walking back to his truck. Splash pulled into the storage lot with Mango right behind her. She stopped at storage unit 49. Splash got out of her car. Her legs were like rubber. Mango parked and got out right behind her and whispered in her ear, "Open it nice and slow." Splash's hands shook violently. She managed to get the lock off and lifted the storage gate. The storage space revealed old furniture and boxes of clothes, two tall cabinets, and two old deep freezers.

"Where the shit at?" Peppay asked, holding a gun on Splash. He was still mad that Splash shot him a few months ago.

"Mango, you said you wouldn't hurt me," Splash said as she stood there in fear.

"I said I wouldn't. Now, where is the product?"

"It's in the deep freezer."

Mango walked over to one of the deep freezers and opened it. Stacks of bricks were nicely stacked on top of each other, with Mango's signature red star stamp on every one of them. Mango smiled. Splash watched Peppay with watery eyes. Just then, a U-Haul pulled up outside of the open storage distracting Mango and Peppay. Giving Velli and E-Moe a chance to step out the cabinets they were hiding in. "Don't move, you Taco Bell eating muthafucka," E-Moe said, putting his gun to the back of Peppay's head. Velli stood smiling, holding Mango at gunpoint. Mario jumped out the U-Haul holding an AR-15.

***

Malaya was mentally in another world. Her situation had her wanting to die. She got up from a late nap, something that she had not done since she had been in C-block. She grabbed her mouthwash and washed up to performed her prayer that she missed due to her being sleep. Malaya patted her thigh to make sure that her ice-pick was still strapped to her leg. She left the cell to see if Angie wanted to pray with her. Angie converted over to Islam a few days ago. Exiting the cell, Jada was sitting Indian style in front of the door reading the USA-Today. "Hey, Malaya," Jada greeted her cellmate.

"Hey, girl. Where is Angie?"

"She was on the top tier sweeping and mopping the corner where you two be praying at. Oh! You know that you are in the newspaper. The prosecutor is predicting that she will convict you," Jada said, getting up from her sitting position.

"Fuck Samantha Davis," Malaya mumbled, reaching the top-tier. Jada and Malaya were met by the Amber Rose look alike. Malaya had found out her name was Candice, and she was the same woman that stared her down in the bullpen the first day she went to court. Candice purposely bumped into Malaya. "Watch where you are goi-" Malaya's words were cut short by Candice's seven- inch shank that sliced into the right side of Malaya's face. Malaya stumbled into Jada, reaching and pulling out her ice-pick. Jada's back was up against the wall.

Malaya made her move for Candice. She swung the ice-pick, stabbing Candice in the shoulder. "Agggg!" Candice cried out in pain. Candice swung for Malaya's face again, but missing it by inches. The unit went in an uproar.

"Get that ass, Malaya!" A group of girls cheered on.

"Fuck that bitch up, Candice." Tiffany and a group of girls rooted for Candice. The women in C-block blocked the entrance of the unit with tables, mattresses, and trash cans. The C.O.'s were fighting to get in the unit to stop the madness. Out of nowhere, Dee-Dee slammed her shank into the back of Malaya's right shoulder. Malaya let out a scream, but she kept on fighting. She started to feel light-headed, but she kept swinging her knife at Candice. She was ready to die, but she wanted to make sure that she took one of those bitches with her. Jada attacked Dee-Dee from behind viciously with her ice-pick, jumping on her back and stabbing her repeatedly in the chest and neck. Dee-Dee flipped her over on the floor, drove her shank into Jada's neck, and broke the weapon off into the wound. Dee-Dee blacked out from her wounds on top of Jada.

Malaya circled around with Candice on wobbly legs. Candice faked an attack and Malaya jumped back. Malaya was waiting for a kill shot, neck shot, or eye shot. She knew that she had to hurt Candice fast. Candice rushed Malaya, causing her to slip on the dark blood that was all over the floor, Candice fell on top of Malaya pushing her blade into Malaya's stomach. The C.O.s were banging on the glass sliding door. "Stop! Drop your weapons! That's an order!" They yelled as they still fought to get into the unit.

Candice sat up on Malaya's stomach with her knife raised in the air. "This is for Keisha, bitch!"

"Get the fuck off her!" Angie screamed as she swung the broken handle of a broom stick, catching Candice in the face with it and knocking her off Malaya. The knife fell out of Candice's hand.

Malaya rolled over on top of Candice. "Kill her ass." The women in the unit coached Malaya. Malaya straddled Candice holding her face back, Malaya repeatedly rammed her ice-pick into Candice's face. The ice-pick put so many holes in Candice's face. Malaya even stabbed her through the tongue.

"Everybody lay down on the ground now!" Tear gas was shot in the air of C-block as the C.O.s finally gained access to C-block. Officer Hightower tackled Malaya off Candice as Malaya blacked out.

Chapter 37

I've waited so long for this day to come," Velli said, pointing his gun at Mango. Everyone was now inside the storage room with the metal gate pulled down.

"So this is how it's going to be mi amigo?" Mango said, looking into the eyes of Velli.

"You brought this one on yourself. You forced me to move drugs for you when I just wanted to live life with my family. You supplied Stone behind my back. You even paid him to kill me."

Mango listened in horror.

"Look, my friend. I'll give you five million dollars just to let me go. I'll deposit it into your account." Velli just smiled.

"You must think all blacks are just that damn greedy, don't you?"

"No, Amigo. Not you," Mango said with his head hung low.

Velli walked over to Splash. Are you ready?" Splash nodded her head up and down. E-Moe handed his gun to her. Splash walked over to Peppay without hesitation, she blew his brains out. This was to ensure that she would always have E-Moe and Velli's protection. Splash pointed the gun at Mango. "No, don't let this whore kill me. You kill me. Puta, mutha-fucka!" Mango yelled, looking at Velli.

"Naw, Slim. She got it." Splash popped two holes in Mango's head. They placed both bodies in the cabinets, taped them closed, and placed them on the back of the U-Haul. E-Moe and Mario rode away with the bodies, and Velli loaded and relocated the drugs. Splash went back to Atlanta with E-Moe. He was her boo.

***

Mr. McCullough sat in his Naples, Florida office building behind his large oak wood desk going over Malaya's case file. He had been going over her case non-stop for the last past four hours. He hated losing in court to those crackers, and it seemed like the courts had set him up to lose. Being though he hadn't heard anything about the murder of a Hillsborough County Police Officer, he knew that Velli had not located the whereabouts of Officer Bernard Grant... "Psss!" McCullough let out a sigh, removed his Prada frames from his face, and pressed down on the bridge of his nose, trying to relieve the tension that was building up in his eyes from reading the extensive paperwork. "These muthafuckas have me by the balls on this one," McCullough spoke aloud.

"Mr. McCullough, you have a call on line 2," The lovely voice of his secretary interrupted Mr. McCullough through the intercom that sat on the corner of his desk.

"Loretta, I told you to hold all of my calls. I don't want to be disturbed."

"I know, and I'm sorry, but the caller on the phone stated that she had some very useful info about the Malaya Williams case." Mr. McCullough perked up hearing Malaya's name.

"Okay. Put her through, Loretta."

"Hello," the soft spoken voice said as Mr. McCullough picked up the phone.

"This is McCullough. How may I help you?" The lady spoke into the phone and McCullough listened to every detail. "Look, Ms. Let's not say anymore over the phone. Let's talk in person." Mr. McCullough jotted down an address and number and hung the phone up. Racing out of the office, he texted Velli and told him to stand down on the Grant issue.

Chapter 38

6 months later… Malaya sat behind the defendant's table at trial. They had to postpone her trial date back due to the medical conditions she sustained at the jail. They just picked their jury of nine white men and three black women. The courtroom was filled with camera crews and news reporters. This was the first time that Judge Karen Jackson allowed the media to be present in her courtroom during a live trial. She wanted to publicly crucify Malaya in front of the whole world. Malaya sat quietly praying, asking Allah to have mercy on her. Mr. McCullough acted like he didn't have a care in the world. Malaya slightly looked over her shoulder and locked eyes with Velli. He mouthed the words, "I Love You" at her.

Tears filled Malaya's eyes as she mouthed the words "I know" back to him. Damu, Anya, and Akeemah sat in the courtroom to show support for their sister. Ms. Samantha Davis began with her case.

"Ladies and gentlemen of the jury, today, I'm going to prove to you that this lady right here-" Ms. Davis pointed a finger at Malaya. "Killed Keisha Timmons in cold blood and with ill intent. Today, you're going to hear about how she hated Keisha Timmons and killed her over a man named Mike Jones. The same man that was murdered in front of Keisha Timmons' apartment the same night Keisha was murdered."

"I object, Your Honor. Mike Jones has nothing to do with this case or my client," Mr. McCullough said, jumping to his feet.

"Overruled," Judge Jackson said without even looking at Mr. McCullough. Ms. Davis went on about Malaya killing Keisha twenty minutes later. Ms. Davis closed her open arguments. Then it was Mr. McCullough's turn to speak on Malaya's behalf. He stood up, fixed his tie, and simply said that

"Talk is cheap" and sat back down and crossed his legs. Malaya looked at him like he was crazy.

"I want to call my first witness to the stand. Iris Timmons." Iris strutted her stuff all the way to the stand, raised her hand to oath, and proceeded to testify. She told the jury how Malaya three years ago attacked Keisha, cutting her face and putting her in a coma because Malaya was jealous over Keisha and Mike's relationship.

"Malaya was upset that Mike rejected her," Iris said, lying through her teeth with a straight face.

"No further questions, Your Honor."

"Mr. McCullough, do you wish to question the witness?" Judge Jackson asked for the bench.

"No, Your Honor." Malaya looked at her lawyer like she could've slap the shit out of him. Mr. McCullough touched her hand and said, "Just relax. I know what I'm doing." He then said, "I'm calling my next witness, Fatima Timmons, Keisha Timmons' mother." The bailiff went to get Fatima from the witness room, but he came back empty handed. He informed Ms. Davis that Fatima Timmons was not in the witness room. "Your Honor, I think that my witness may have stepped to the ladies room. Can I please go ahead with my other witness and come back to Fatima Timmons later?"

"Yes, you may," Judge Jackson replied.

"I'm calling Officer Bernard Grant to the stand." The bailiff came back with Officer Grant. He was decked out in his service uniform. He took oath and sat on the stand.

"Mr. Grant, were you present the night Keisha Timmons was murdered?" Ms. Davis asked from behind the prosecutor table.

"Yes, I was."

"And, were you alone?"

"Yes, I was." Officer Grant nodded his head up and down as he spoke.

"Do you see the person that killed Ms. Keisha Timmons?"

"Yes, I do. She is sitting right over there with that thing wrapped around her head." Officer Grant pointed out.

"Okay, tell us what you witnessed the night that Keisha was killed."

I was sitting on a back street maybe two or three blocks away from Mulberry Drive filling out some paperwork. When out of nowhere, this young lady came chasing behind Keisha Timmons with a gun and shot her."

Loud chatter erupted in the courtroom.

"Quiet, please. Order in the court!" Judge Jackson yelled, quieting her courtroom.

"Did Keisha Timmons have a gun?" Ms. Davis asked, already knowing the answer.

"No, there wasn't a gun except for the one that I recovered from Malaya which was used to kill Ms. Timmons," Officer Grant stated with a straight face.

"Okay, I have no further questions, Your Honor." Ms. Davis sat down in her chair.

"Do you want to question Officer Grant?" Judge Jackson asked Mr. McCullough.

"Yes, Your Honor. I would." Mr. McCullough stood up and buttoned his Tom Ford jacket.

"Mr. Grant, I'm going to give you one chance to come clean and tell the jury that you are a liar." The courtroom went into a frenzy.

"Order in the court." Judge Jackson banged her gavel. The courtroom fell silent.

"Mr. McCullough, one more outburst like that, and I'm going to hold you in contempt."

"Okay, Your Honor, no further questions," Mr. McCullough said as he sat back in his chair. The government went on to rest their case. Ms. Fatima was nowhere to be found. The prosecutor thought that she still could get a conviction without the help of Fatima Timmons.

Chapter 39

The courts took a five minute break, then they allowed Mr. McCullough to put on his case for the jury. "Your Honor, I would like to call my witness Nicole Dickens to the stand." The blond bombshell tip toed her way to the stand in 7-inch high heels and a leopard print mini skirt. The skirt was so short that you could almost see her milky ass cheeks if she bent or moved the wrong way. She took the oath and took a seat on the stand.

"Okay, Ms. Dickens. Can you please tell the jury what it is that you do for a living?" Mr. McCullough asked.

"I'm a prostitute." Malaya looked at her lawyer like he had lost his damn mind.

"Have you ever seen this woman that's sitting next to me before?"

"Yes, I have," Ms. Dickens replied, leaning forward and speaking directly into the microphone that was in front of her.

"And could you please tell us where you have seen my client?" Mr. McCullough said as he got up and started to pace in front of the jury box.

"I saw her on the TV on the news."

"And have you seen her any other place besides the news?"

"I saw her the night Keisha Timmons was killed."

"I object, Your Honor! There's no proof of this," Ms. Davis said, jumping to her feet.

"Overruled," Judge Jackson replied from the bench. Ms. Davis flopped down in her chair and McCullough continued cross examining his witness.

"Let's back up for minute. Ms. Dickens, do you know an Officer Grant that works for The Hillsborough County Police Department?"

"Yes, I do."

"Could you please tell us where do you know Officer Grant from?"

"He's a regular John that comes to trick with me." The courtroom buzzed with noise. Judge Jackson gave the occupants a stern look and they became silent.

"Were you with Officer Grant the night that Keisha Timmons was murdered?" Mr. McCullough questioned Ms. Dickens calmly.

"Yes, sir. I was with Officer Grant the night Keisha was killed."

"Tell the ladies and gentlemen of the jury what you and Officer Grant were doing, and how was it that you came to see Keisha Timmons' murder."

"Well, like I said, I had been turning tricks with Officer Grant for a while. Me and my pimp, Pretty Ricky, decided we were going to blackmail Officer Grant by videotaping me servicing him without him knowing it." Officer Grant sat in the back of the courtroom tight faced. Hearing Nicole's whore ass expose who he really was. "I wore a hidden camera on my necklace that I got at the spy shop. You couldn't even tell that I was wearing a camera. I was in Officer Grant's patrol car giving him oral pleasure when I heard him say, "Oh shit!" and jolted in his seat. When I raised my head out of Officer Grant's lap to see what got him all worked up, I saw Keisha Timmons pull a gun on that lady right there." Ms. Dickens pointed a finger at Malaya. "Then I saw Mrs. Williams pull her gun and shoot Mrs. Timmons in the head." The courtroom erupted in chaos.

"Quiet, please." Judge Jackson stood up behind the bench and viciously banged her gavel.

"Your Honor, I would like to submit into evidence exhibit A. It's a video of the murder of Keisha Timmons," Mr. McCullough said with a smile on his face.

"The court notes that Mr. McCullough submitted exhibit A into evidence." Judge Jackson rolled her eyes at Mr. McCullough.

Mr. McCullough hit play on the overhead projector that was placed in the courtroom for his use. The image of the video showed Nicole Dickens performing oral sex on Officer Grant. You could clearly hear Officer Grant saying the words, "Oh shit!" Then, Keisha and Malaya came into view on the large screen. Keisha pointed her gun and so did Malaya. You could see Malaya's gun discharge in her hand and blow a perfect nickel sized hole in her forehead. "Get the fuck out of here!" Officer Grant said to Miss Dickens on camera. The screen showed that Officer Grant approached Malaya with his weapon drawn telling her to lay down on the ground. After he handcuffed Malaya, he walked over to Keisha's body, picked her gun up, and placed it in his pocket. At that moment, you could see images of a female image running, which proved that Miss Dickens ran away from the crime scene. The courtroom was dead silent. The prosecutor sat at her table with her head down.

"Your Honor, I would like at this time to submit a motion to have all charges against my client dismissed due to Officer Grant withholding valuable evidence, giving false statements to the courts, and for Officer Grant being a corrupted cop. I want this court to launch a full investigation on Officer Grant at this time," Mr. McCullough said with a devilish grin and he straightened out his tie. Judge Jackson looked like she was going to have a heart attack.

"Does the prosecution object to Mr. McCullough's motion to dismiss?" Judge Jackson asked Ms. Davis. Ms. Davis forcefully threw papers into her briefcase.

"No, Your Honor. I do not object."

"This court grants Mr. McCullough motion for dismissal. Mrs. Williams, you are free to go." The court burst into chaos. Malaya was still seated at the defense table in a daze. She couldn't believe that the judge just said that she was a free woman. Anya and Akeemah jumped the divider and bear hugged their sister in faith. Walking Malaya into the hallway of the courtroom, Velli was waiting. He and Malaya's eyes met for the second time of that day. Malaya ran to him jumping in his arms and wrapping her legs around him. "Oh, baby. I love you," Malaya said, breaking down crying in her husband's arms.

"I love you too, baby. I thought that I lost you," Velli admitted, tightly squeezing Malaya.

"Come on. Let's go make a statement to the press," Mr. McCullough said, leading the way to the front of the court building. Flashes of lights hit them as they exited the court building and found their way to the side walk where the press was set up. Velli had his arm held tightly around Malaya with Damu and Anya standing with them. Mr. McCullough smiled for the cameras and straightened his tie. "Justice has been served," McCullough said into the mic that was in front of him.

"Justice is not served!" Officer Grant screamed out.

"He has a gun!" one of the news reporters shouted out. Officer Grant lifted his gun, aimed it at Malaya, and opened fire. Velli pushed Malaya to the ground covering her with his body. It seemed like fifty shots were fired before the shooting stopped. Two officers gunned down Officer Grant before he could hit his target. Velli rolled off of his wife and checked her for any wounds. He was thankful that she wasn't hurt.

Jibril Williams

Epilogue

Malaya stood looking down at the headstone that was at her feet. She missed Jada so much. There was so much that she wanted to do with Jada before her illness took its toll on her. Malaya wiped tears from her cheeks. "I will never forget you, Jada. I promise," Malaya whispered.

Malaya felt that Jada saved her life and she was forever indebted to Jada for that. She was happy to be free, but was so sad to lose someone like Jada. She and Velli put the past behind them. Anya showed Malaya the complete footage of the video that Yvette made of her and Velli. The video showed Velli rejecting Yvette. Velli saved Malaya from spending the rest of her life in prison. Velli brought Nicole Dickens' testimony and video of the murder for $100,000. He did that knowing that Malaya didn't want anything to do with him.

"Oh, Allah. Please be good to her. She was one of those who deserves it," Malaya spoke in a whisper. "I love you, Jada." Two small figures walked up beside Malaya. The two girls looked like identical angels, despite the burned mark that one of them had.

"Hey, Crystal and Cristian," Malaya greeted Jada's daughters. The two little girls smiled their brightest smile at Malaya as they laid flowers on their mother's grave. Malaya and Velli adopted the two girls. Malaya wanted to give them the best life possible. Jada's mother agreed to it. Malaya grabbed the two little girls' hands and walked to the trucks where Velli, Damu, Anya, and Akeemah were waiting to relocate and start a new life together.

***

Hakeem laid prostrating at the Masjid, praying to his Lord. He read Keisha's diary and couldn't do anything, but accept that her malicious ways got her in her situation. Therefore, he found forgiveness in his heart for Malaya and Velli. After all, he wanted his Lord to forgive him for his sins, so he had to be willing to forgive others.

The End

Lock Down Publications and Ca$h Presents assisted publishing packages.

BASIC PACKAGE $499
Editing
Cover Design
Formatting

UPGRADED PACKAGE $800
Typing
Editing
Cover Design
Formatting

ADVANCE PACKAGE $1,200
Typing
Editing
Cover Design
Formatting
Copyright registration
Proofreading
Upload book to Amazon

LDP SUPREME PACKAGE $1,500
Typing
Editing
Cover Design
Formatting
Copyright registration

Proofreading
Set up Amazon account
Upload book to Amazon
Advertise on LDP Amazon and Facebook page

***Other services available upon request. Additional
charges may apply
Lock Down Publications
P.O. Box 944
Stockbridge, GA 30281-9998
Phone # 470 303-9761

Submission Guideline

Submit the first three chapters of your completed manuscript to ldpsubmissions@gmail.com, subject line: Your book's title. The manuscript must be in a .doc file and sent as an attachment. Document should be in Times New Roman, double spaced and in size 12 font. Also, provide your synopsis and full contact information. If sending multiple submissions, they must each be in a separate email.

Have a story but no way to send it electronically? You can still submit to LDP/Ca$h Presents. Send in the first three chapters, written or typed, of your completed manuscript to:

LDP: Submissions Dept
Po Box 944
Stockbridge, Ga 30281

DO NOT send original manuscript. Must be a duplicate.

Provide your synopsis and a cover letter containing your full contact information.

Thanks for considering LDP and Ca$h Presents.

<u>NEW RELEASES</u>

TIL DEATH by ARYANNA
IT'S JUST ME AND YOU by AH'MILLION
QUEEN OF THE ZOO 2 by BLACK MIGO
THE HEART OF A SAVAGE 4 by JIBRIL WIL-
LIAMS
THE BIRTH OF A GANGSTER 2 by DEL-
MONT PLAYER
LOYAL TO THE SOIL 3 by JIBRIL WILLIAMS

By **T.J. Edwards**

GORILLAZ IN THE BAY V

3X KRAZY III

STRAIGHT BEAST MODE III

De'Kari

KINGPIN KILLAZ IV

STREET KINGS III

PAID IN BLOOD III

CARTEL KILLAZ IV

DOPE GODS III

Hood Rich

SINS OF A HUSTLA II

ASAD

RICH $AVAGE II

By Martell Troublesome Bolden

YAYO V

Bred In The Game 2

S. Allen

CREAM III

THE STREETS WILL TALK II

By Yolanda Moore

SON OF A DOPE FIEND III

HEAVEN GOT A GHETTO II

By Renta

LOYALTY AIN'T PROMISED III

By Keith Williams

I'M NOTHING WITHOUT HIS LOVE II

SINS OF A THUG II

TO THE THUG I LOVED BEFORE II

IN A HUSTLER I TRUST II

By Monet Dragun

QUIET MONEY IV

EXTENDED CLIP III

THUG LIFE IV

By **Trai'Quan**

THE STREETS MADE ME IV

By **Larry D. Wright**

IF YOU CROSS ME ONCE II

ANGEL IV

By **Anthony Fields**

THE STREETS WILL NEVER CLOSE IV

By K'ajji

HARD AND RUTHLESS III

KILLA KOUNTY III

By Khufu

MONEY GAME III

By Smoove Dolla

JACK BOYS VS DOPE BOYS II

A GANGSTA'S QUR'AN V

COKE GIRLZ II

By Romell Tukes

MURDA WAS THE CASE II

Elijah R. Freeman

THE STREETS NEVER LET GO II

By Robert Baptiste

AN UNFORESEEN LOVE III

By **Meesha**

KING OF THE TRENCHES III

by **GHOST & TRANAY ADAMS**

MONEY MAFIA II

By **Jibril Williams**

QUEEN OF THE ZOO III

By **Black Migo**

VICIOUS LOYALTY III

By Kingpen

A GANGSTA'S PAIN III

By J-Blunt

CONFESSIONS OF A JACKBOY III

By Nicholas Lock

GRIMEY WAYS II

By Ray Vinci

KING KILLA II

By Vincent "Vitto" Holloway

BETRAYAL OF A THUG II

By Fre$h

THE MURDER QUEENS II

By Michael Gallon

THE BIRTH OF A GANGSTER III

By Delmont Player

TREAL LOVE II

By Le'Monica Jackson

FOR THE LOVE OF BLOOD II
By Jamel Mitchell
RAN OFF ON DA PLUG II
By Paper Boi Rari
HOOD CONSIGLIERE II
By Keese
PRETTY GIRLS DO NASTY THINGS II
By Nicole Goosby
PROTÉGÉ OF A LEGEND II
By Corey Robinson
IT'S JUST ME AND YOU II
By Ah'Million

Available Now

RESTRAINING ORDER **I & II**
By **CA$H & Coffee**
LOVE KNOWS NO BOUNDARIES **I II & III**
By **Coffee**
RAISED AS A GOON I, II, III & IV
BRED BY THE SLUMS I, II, III
BLAST FOR ME I & II
ROTTEN TO THE CORE I II III
A BRONX TALE I, II, III

DUFFLE BAG CARTEL I II III IV V VI

HEARTLESS GOON I II III IV V

A SAVAGE DOPEBOY I II

DRUG LORDS I II III

CUTTHROAT MAFIA I II

KING OF THE TRENCHES

By **Ghost**

LAY IT DOWN **I & II**

LAST OF A DYING BREED I II

BLOOD STAINS OF A SHOTTA I & II III

By **Jamaica**

LOYAL TO THE GAME I II III

LIFE OF SIN I, II III

By **TJ & Jelissa**

BLOODY COMMAS I & II

SKI MASK CARTEL I II & III

KING OF NEW YORK I II,III IV V

RISE TO POWER I II III

COKE KINGS I II III IV V

BORN HEARTLESS I II III IV

KING OF THE TRAP I II

By **T.J. Edwards**

IF LOVING HIM IS WRONG…I & II

LOVE ME EVEN WHEN IT HURTS I II III

By **Jelissa**

WHEN THE STREETS CLAP BACK I & II III

THE HEART OF A SAVAGE I II III IV

MONEY MAFIA

LOYAL TO THE SOIL I II III

By **Jibril Williams**

A DISTINGUISHED THUG STOLE MY HEART I II & III

LOVE SHOULDN'T HURT I II III IV

RENEGADE BOYS I II III IV

PAID IN KARMA I II III

SAVAGE STORMS I II III

AN UNFORESEEN LOVE I II

By **Meesha**

A GANGSTER'S CODE I &, II III

A GANGSTER'S SYN I II III

THE SAVAGE LIFE I II III

CHAINED TO THE STREETS I II III

BLOOD ON THE MONEY I II III

A GANGSTA'S PAIN I II

By **J-Blunt**

PUSH IT TO THE LIMIT

By **Bre' Hayes**

BLOOD OF A BOSS **I, II, III, IV, V**

SHADOWS OF THE GAME

TRAP BASTARD

By **Askari**

THE STREETS BLEED MURDER **I, II & III**

THE HEART OF A GANGSTA I II& III

By **Jerry Jackson**

CUM FOR ME I II III IV V VI VII VIII

Jibril Williams

An **LDP Erotica Collaboration**
BRIDE OF A HUSTLA **I II & II**
THE FETTI GIRLS **I, II& III**
CORRUPTED BY A GANGSTA I, II III, IV
BLINDED BY HIS LOVE
THE PRICE YOU PAY FOR LOVE I, II ,III
DOPE GIRL MAGIC I II III
By **Destiny Skai**
WHEN A GOOD GIRL GOES BAD
By **Adrienne**
THE COST OF LOYALTY I II III
By Kweli
A GANGSTER'S REVENGE **I II III & IV**
THE BOSS MAN'S DAUGHTERS I II III IV V
A SAVAGE LOVE **I & II**
BAE BELONGS TO ME I II
A HUSTLER'S DECEIT I, II, III
WHAT BAD BITCHES DO I, II, III
SOUL OF A MONSTER I II III
KILL ZONE
A DOPE BOY'S QUEEN I II III
TIL DEATH
By **Aryanna**
A KINGPIN'S AMBITON
A KINGPIN'S AMBITION **II**
I MURDER FOR THE DOUGH
By **Ambitious**

174

TRUE SAVAGE I II III IV V VI VII
DOPE BOY MAGIC I, II, III
MIDNIGHT CARTEL I II III
CITY OF KINGZ I II
NIGHTMARE ON SILENT AVE
THE PLUG OF LIL MEXICO II
CLASSIC CITY
By **Chris Green**
A DOPEBOY'S PRAYER
By **Eddie "Wolf" Lee**
THE KING CARTEL **I, II & III**
By **Frank Gresham**
THESE NIGGAS AIN'T LOYAL **I, II & III**
By **Nikki Tee**
GANGSTA SHYT **I II &III**
By **CATO**
THE ULTIMATE BETRAYAL
By **Phoenix**
BOSS'N UP **I , II & III**
By **Royal Nicole**
I LOVE YOU TO DEATH
By **Destiny J**
I RIDE FOR MY HITTA
I STILL RIDE FOR MY HITTA
By **Misty Holt**
LOVE & CHASIN' PAPER
By **Qay Crockett**

TO DIE IN VAIN

SINS OF A HUSTLA

By **ASAD**

BROOKLYN HUSTLAZ

By **Boogsy Morina**

BROOKLYN ON LOCK I & II

By **Sonovia**

GANGSTA CITY

By **Teddy Duke**

A DRUG KING AND HIS DIAMOND I & II III

A DOPEMAN'S RICHES

HER MAN, MINE'S TOO I, II

CASH MONEY HO'S

THE WIFEY I USED TO BE I II

PRETTY GIRLS DO NASTY THINGS

By Nicole Goosby

TRAPHOUSE KING **I II & III**

KINGPIN KILLAZ I II III

STREET KINGS I II

PAID IN BLOOD **I II**

CARTEL KILLAZ I II III

DOPE GODS I II

By **Hood Rich**

LIPSTICK KILLAH **I, II, III**

CRIME OF PASSION I II & III

FRIEND OR FOE I II III

By **Mimi**

STEADY MOBBN' **I, II, III**

THE STREETS STAINED MY SOUL I II III

By **Marcellus Allen**

WHO SHOT YA **I, II, III**

SON OF A DOPE FIEND I II

HEAVEN GOT A GHETTO

Renta

GORILLAZ IN THE BAY **I II III IV**

TEARS OF A GANGSTA I II

3X KRAZY I II

STRAIGHT BEAST MODE I II

DE'KARI

TRIGGADALE I II III

MURDAROBER WAS THE CASE

Elijah R. Freeman

GOD BLESS THE TRAPPERS I, II, III

THESE SCANDALOUS STREETS I, II, III

FEAR MY GANGSTA I, II, III IV, V

THESE STREETS DON'T LOVE NOBODY I, II

BURY ME A G I, II, III, IV, V

A GANGSTA'S EMPIRE I, II, III, IV

THE DOPEMAN'S BODYGAURD I II

THE REALEST KILLAZ I II III

THE LAST OF THE OGS I II III

Tranay Adams

THE STREETS ARE CALLING

Duquie Wilson

MARRIED TO A BOSS I II III
By Destiny Skai & Chris Green
KINGZ OF THE GAME I II III IV V VI
Playa Ray
SLAUGHTER GANG I II III
RUTHLESS HEART I II III
By Willie Slaughter
FUK SHYT
By Blakk Diamond
DON'T F#CK WITH MY HEART I II
By Linnea
ADDICTED TO THE DRAMA I II III
IN THE ARM OF HIS BOSS II
By Jamila
YAYO I II III IV
A SHOOTER'S AMBITION I II
BRED IN THE GAME
By S. Allen
TRAP GOD I II III
RICH $AVAGE
MONEY IN THE GRAVE I II III
By Martell Troublesome Bolden
FOREVER GANGSTA
GLOCKS ON SATIN SHEETS I II
By Adrian Dulan
TOE TAGZ I II III IV
LEVELS TO THIS SHYT I II

IT'S JUST ME AND YOU

By Ah'Million

KINGPIN DREAMS I II III

RAN OFF ON DA PLUG

By Paper Boi Rari

CONFESSIONS OF A GANGSTA I II III IV

CONFESSIONS OF A JACKBOY I II

By Nicholas Lock

I'M NOTHING WITHOUT HIS LOVE

SINS OF A THUG

TO THE THUG I LOVED BEFORE

A GANGSTA SAVED XMAS

IN A HUSTLER I TRUST

By Monet Dragun

CAUGHT UP IN THE LIFE I II III

THE STREETS NEVER LET GO

By Robert Baptiste

NEW TO THE GAME I II III

MONEY, MURDER & MEMORIES I II III

By **Malik D. Rice**

LIFE OF A SAVAGE I II III

A GANGSTA'S QUR'AN I II III IV

MURDA SEASON I II III

GANGLAND CARTEL I II III

CHI'RAQ GANGSTAS I II III

KILLERS ON ELM STREET I II III

JACK BOYZ N DA BRONX I II III

A DOPEBOY'S DREAM I II III

JACK BOYS VS DOPE BOYS

COKE GIRLZ

By Romell Tukes

LOYALTY AIN'T PROMISED I II

By Keith Williams

QUIET MONEY I II III

THUG LIFE I II III

EXTENDED CLIP I II

By **Trai'Quan**

THE STREETS MADE ME I II III

By **Larry D. Wright**

THE ULTIMATE SACRIFICE I, II, III, IV, V, VI

KHADIFI

IF YOU CROSS ME ONCE

ANGEL I II III

IN THE BLINK OF AN EYE

By **Anthony Fields**

THE LIFE OF A HOOD STAR

By Ca$h & Rashia Wilson

THE STREETS WILL NEVER CLOSE I II III

By K'ajji

CREAM I II

THE STREETS WILL TALK

By Yolanda Moore

NIGHTMARES OF A HUSTLA I II III

By King Dream

CONCRETE KILLA I II III
VICIOUS LOYALTY I II
By Kingpen
HARD AND RUTHLESS I II
MOB TOWN 251
THE BILLIONAIRE BENTLEYS I II III
By Von Diesel
GHOST MOB
Stilloan Robinson
MOB TIES I II III IV V VI
By SayNoMore
BODYMORE MURDERLAND I II III
THE BIRTH OF A GANGSTER I II
By Delmont Player
FOR THE LOVE OF A BOSS
By C. D. Blue
MOBBED UP I II III IV
THE BRICK MAN I II III IV
THE COCAINE PRINCESS I II III IV V
By King Rio
KILLA KOUNTY I II III
By Khufu
MONEY GAME I II
By Smoove Dolla
A GAÑGSTA'S KARMA I II
By FLAME
KING OF THE TRENCHES I II

by **GHOST & TRANAY ADAMS**

QUEEN OF THE ZOO I II

By **Black Migo**

GRIMEY WAYS

By Ray Vinci

XMAS WITH AN ATL SHOOTER

By Ca$h & Destiny Skai

KING KILLA

By Vincent "Vitto" Holloway

BETRAYAL OF A THUG

By Fre$h

THE MURDER QUEENS

By Michael Gallon

TREAL LOVE

By Le'Monica Jackson

FOR THE LOVE OF BLOOD

By Jamel Mitchell

HOOD CONSIGLIERE

By Keese

PROTÉGÉ OF A LEGEND

By Corey Robinson

BOOKS BY LDP'S CEO, CA$H

TRUST IN NO MAN

TRUST IN NO MAN 2

TRUST IN NO MAN 3

BONDED BY BLOOD

SHORTY GOT A THUG

THUGS CRY

THUGS CRY 2

THUGS CRY 3

TRUST NO BITCH

TRUST NO BITCH 2

TRUST NO BITCH 3

TIL MY CASKET DROPS

RESTRAINING ORDER

RESTRAINING ORDER 2

IN LOVE WITH A CONVICT

LIFE OF A HOOD STAR

XMAS WITH AN ATL SHOOTER

Jibril Williams

CPSIA information can be obtained
at www.ICGtesting.com
Printed in the USA
LVHW081100290822
727089LV00007B/108

9 781955 270946